Senso Unico

(Life is a One Way Street)

To Nick,
Hope you enjoy this!
love Dad x

By

– P J MASCALL –

An environmentally friendly book printed and bound in England by
www.printondemand-worldwide.com

This book is made entirely of chain-of-custody materials

www.fast-print.net/store.php

Senso Unico
Copyright © P J Mascall 2011

All rights reserved

No part of this book may be reproduced in any form by photocopying or any electronic or mechanical means, including information storage or retrieval systems, without permission in writing from both the copyright owner and the publisher of the book.

ISBN 978-178035-097-4

First published 2011 by
FASTPRINT PUBLISHING
Peterborough, England.

Senso Unico

I dedicate this work to the memory of Toby Mascall 1921-1999 & my dear mother Sylvia 1927-2002.

Davide's character was inspired by my close friend Davide Moriconi.

P J Mascall

Introduction.

Tino Citraro, an old Genoan raised in the port area known by its old Genoano name of the "Caruggi"[1], returns to retell of a summer of emotion and disaster. It was a summer that would change the lives of two of his dearest friends forever. Cinzia and Davide's tragedy would begin to haunt him again as he remembers a world that changed their lives forever. After meeting his beloved Cinzia, now an old lady living in the same house she occupied as a young girl, the past is once more unravelled!

Tino was now an old man in his late seventies and Cinzia a few years older. He was a retired advertisement salesman that had spent most of his working life living in exile in the United States after an influential period on the beautiful Island of Sardinia. Cinzia was about four years his senior yet, despite the

---

[1] The name Caruggi is Genoese and not Italian.

fifty year gap that had elapsed, both recall with vivid imagination the events of that long, hot, post-war summer. Perhaps, even now after so many years, the events that took place in the Autumn of their childhood can finally be buried, and the tragedy that was Cinzia and Davide's can finally be put to rest? Theirs was a story of innocence, of growing, of desperation and love.

There are a few surprises in store for Tino in his search for peace of mind, as he reflects on a time when evil men wielded their influence on those in most need.

Senso Unico is a story set in the the time of Neo-Realist Cinema, of gangster films, of political turmoil, of corruption, and above all, poverty. In post war Genoa everyone spoke in a Genoese dialect in those times and Italian was hardly ever used[2]. Two teenage boys, Tino and Davide, lived out their adventurous youth in the war ravaged city, until one day, their lives are changed forever in a slit second of madness.

---

[2] Only with the advent of television did the Italian language really take over from the many dialects spoken throughout the peninsular.

Senso Unico

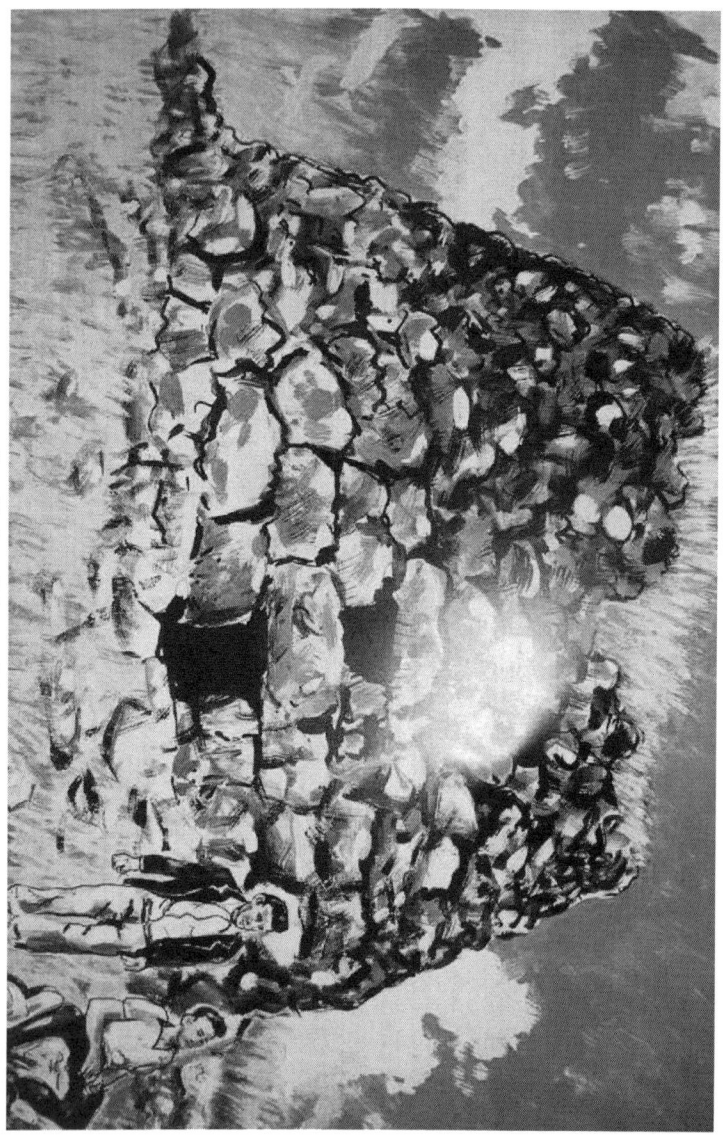

Sardinian Nuraghi

Chapter One: The Return.

Some things never change. The street was still too steep to walk on, and the old port was still visible between the tall murky buildings. Only I had changed, I had finally grown old and become like all of those old men that sit in the square and talk about their younger days, how they had opposed the Communists, how they had hated Marinetti and how they were liberated by those wonderful Americans. Yes, the war and that era seemed to dominate their chatter and now and it filled my thoughts too.

I was only thirteen years old when the war ended in 1945. These ghettos bring it all back to me now. When I look along the old street I can still see my old pals kicking that big leather football, fighting and shouting as young boys do. I really can still hear their laughter and still see their grubby little faces. How time passes, It all seems like only yesterday. After the war was over Italy lived in a mire of pretence. All was well they said.

Things are getting better. But, especially for those living in these streets, things were getting worse. There was little work to be had and the people were starving. We had old shoes and resorted to petty thieving to survive. The ones who lived better, or so it seemed, were the prostitutes that patrolled the old harbour in late evenings. Genoa was never short of visiting seamen willing to spend and, for a while at least, forget the home they had left behind.

For several minutes I stared at the old green door that once served as the entrance to my mother's old apartment. It looked as though it had never been painted, the green flaked across the wooden panelling that showed through like islands in a seaweed sea. The street, Vico[3] Nievo, was very narrow, and in the evenings quiet dark. Only one gas lamp, which always seemed too dim, made a feeble attempt to light the whole street. The old lamp was still there, like a monument to the past, now accompanied by two yellow coloured, and much taller, posts that looked out of character with their surroundings. The street was still cobbled though, though many cobbles had been replaced and appeared to have a wash of cement to give them an original feel! I looked skywards, toward a sea of shuttered windows. They too were mostly green. There must have been an abundance of green paint at the end of the war I thought. I looked up towards our old kitchen window and for a moment I thought I heard Mama calling me in. Tino-Tino! No I really did

---

[3] Narrow streets (like alleyways)

hear someone. An old lady looked out of the window opposite and called "it's you isn't it?" She looked excited and shouted "wait there - don't go away!". Then she disappeared from the window. I waited and thought that there was something in the voice. Something from the past. Something haunting about her face. But surely Cinzia would not be living in the same house? Could she?.

After a few minutes the old lady appeared at the door. She looked straight into my eyes and I knew immediately it was her. She still looked like an angel to me. The kindest friend I ever had. Older than me by about four years I think. She looked smaller, but then again, old people do don't they? But through the wrinkled, tanned face, I saw a women unchanged by the hard life we had all lived. She slowly raised her arms and wrapped them around my shoulders. There was no traditional kiss - just a long embrace with her head pushed into my chest, where my beating heart gave away my joy.

"I was watching you staring at the door and I knew straight away it was my little Tino" she said. Then she took my hand and with a big smile said "come in Tino - I want to know everything about you". However I felt that the real story was hers. What happened to everyone?, what had she done with her life?, does she have children?. My life as a bachelor, working as an advertisement salesman in the United States for more years than I can remember would surely be less interesting than the marvels she must surely reveal!

We entered the building, which mirrored the old house I once lived in, and climbed the two flights of marbled stairs. "We have a cleaner in now - twice a week to clean these" she said. As we climbed her grip grew tighter. She was clearly very frail and took each step carefully. Then we came to her apartment. I had only just realised that every door, just like those shutters, was green. Did we ever have paint in the war I asked myself, the subject now dominating my thoughts, I really can't remember. I knew the apartment well. Now old photos filled the walls and I noticed among them the smiling face of the parish priest Father Marco. There were also photographs of young children and an old man with a big toothy grin. We crossed the living room and moved into the kitchen where we sat at a huge wooden table. Cinzia turned off the television and turned to me saying with a sigh "my little Tino-how time passes us by" and she was right.

Cinzia still radiated that beauty I remember from long ago. Her high cheek bones, sparkling eyes and radiant smile betrayed her identity. Before me sat a woman who was the victim of her innocence. Cinzia was to us what Beatrice was to Dante and I thanked God to have found her once more.

In those far off days just after the war Cinzia often worked, without pay I might add, with the local priest, Father Marco Albanese, or simply Father Marco to all who knew him. She did everything for that man, made his coffee, cooked his meals, tidied the house, and still had time to joke and have fun with the whole gang of ruffians that hung around the Caruggi, and, it was understood, that she also worked at some late night coffee bar in the nearby suburb of Nervi.

The Caruggi was the old Genoese name for those ancient narrow streets around the old harbour. Usually they were no more than ten feet across. My mother once told me that they were built so close so that if ever the city was invaded, everyone could escape through windows into the next house. I really don't know if that is true, but I always believed it so. It was then as it is now. The streets were always dirty and the smell of fresh fish, wafting in from the port and fish markets, permeated the air. The roads were made up of sets of large square stones, many of which had come lose. The walls were plastered in a grey cement that often disguised the palace within. Most of the doors and shuttered windows were painted in that all too familiar deep green paint.

La Chiesa di Santa Maria was our parish church and it too was dwarfed by the surrounding narrow streets. Like many of the apartment blocks it was an ugly building on the outside, but inside this church would shine with golden statues of the Saints. It was cold looking with its polished marble and was lit with rows of burning candles, which gave the paintings that hung above them a dark and dismal appearance. This was my church, where I was baptised, where I was confirmed a Catholic and where I attended Mass every Sunday without fail!.

It was like the Kasbah in the Caruggi, you could walk in and never come out again. Always walking down a maze of one way streets that never really saw the light of day. Yet these ghettos hid a character, a beauty, a brotherhood, name it what you will, that bonded all those who lived there.

In the warm summer evenings the old folk would sit out in the small square and gossip away their days. They spoke much of the war. Some believed that Mussolini had actually got things right, but he made a few mistakes on the way. Some had once been Communists...at least until the Americans arrived. Then they miraculously changed to anti-Communists that never really wanted Mussolini in the first place!

In the Caruggi the black market flourished. After dark they used to sit around a stove, crudely erected alongside their make-shift stalls, to keep warm on winter evenings. Some would sell water melons, or records, and some cigarettes. The popular cheap brand of cigarette was MS, which many claimed stood for Morto Sicuro![4] Even today the black market thrives, though many of the stalls now sell pornography and CDs, and under the old loose cobbles lie the favourite hiding places for drug dealers.

Hidden in the shadows of the Caruggi, lurking like the shades in Dante's Inferno, was an endless stream of prostitutes, all plying their wares to the foreign seamen that came and went like the seasons. Many of them

---

[4] Morto Sicuro: Lit; death assured.

were young girls of no more than sixteen. Some were old and experienced...and cheaper of course! They were even to be found in Vico Nievo, standing under that lonely old gas lamp.

Genoese life revolved around the old port. This was where the heart of the city beat. The city's most famous sailor had been the legendary Cristofero Colombo[5] and we were always a seafaring race. The Genoese are a proud people, and many of them, like the urchins of Vico Nievo, like even Cristofero, longed for the adventure that only the sea could offer. However, many, like my beloved friend Cinzia, would never leave. Genoa would become her Alcatraz with her dreams of escaping tied to a ball and chain, at the beck and call of evil men. Then again, who am I to talk, I too have returned to a place where my deepest emotions and my fondest memories haunt my thoughts to this, the autumn of my days. I stared at Cinzia and thanked God to have found her again. We talked into the late evening, holding hands, tears welling in our eyes, laughing and smiling. Those tears betrayed the reality of the hard life we had both to endure in our youth. It is so strange how even the smallest detail returns when you can actually openly speak with someone who, like yourself, was raised in the Caruggi.

---

[5] Christopher Columbus who discovered the New World in 1492.

San Giorgio today. Behind this old building lies the area known as the Caruggi.

Chapter Two:
The Urchins of Vico Nievo.

I recall the summers best of all. On these warm evenings, post 1945, we would all go down to the rocks close to the harbour. We loved to call the sea here black water, seeing as we swam in the dark most of the time. Late evening swimming was, after all, a daring pastime! Our favourite spot was the nearby village of Bocadasse, which had a small beach circled by small whitewashed houses. On the beach was always a line of boats, some overturned, that we would play in. In truth the beach was dirty and an old rusting sewer pipe ran down into the bay. Quite how far out it went I will never know but I recall Davide, a dear friend that would shape my future, telling me that if you were drowning and you saw a passing log, never ever grab it!. We all knew exactly what he meant.

It was in many ways a poor man's Santa Margherita, and for all its faults we loved it. We would sit around talking on the sand until the sun went down, and then we would swim in the cool water. Sometimes I was a afraid of swimming there, mainly due to the fact that someone once told me that a great white shark was once spotted in the bay. But my fondest memories were of those long hot summers in Bocadasse.

Of all my friends the one that made us all laugh the most was without doubt one Davide Benotti. He was a blonde haired boy that resembled an Englishman more than any Italian. Davide's poor father had been killed on the Russian front during the war. His father had once written to him saying that "many Italian soldiers didn't even have shoes to wear in the winter". I don't know if what he was saying was the truth, but if it was, his hatred of Mussolini was understandable. His father had written many letters about his time in Russia. Mostly he had complained about the conditions and the weather, and how much he wanted the war to end and get home. In his last letter he spoke about a friend of his, Vilfredo, who was observing the enemy through binoculars when a bullet had passed straight through the lens and took the back of his head off! Davide loved to pass on his father's war stories which he told with sadness and with pride.

Davide lived alone with his mother, a woman who sang like an angel, and longed to go, or escape might be a better word, to America. I am sure that she could have sang in an opera and she would have been at home on the stage of the Carlo Felice Theatre in Genoa's centre.

"I will do it you know, go to America, just you wait!" he always said.

It was strange really, only now did I realise that he must have had a difficult life, and yet, his wonderful sense of mischief covered all the cracks. To me he was the master of the joke and I can never remember him stop laughing. His party trick was to roll backwards with his backside in the air, pass wind and light it with a lighter. It was like a flame thrower and no-one could do it better than him! Once he even burned his arse quite badly and was rubbing cream into it for a week. He could be aggravating too, tweaking your ear as you tried to hold a conversation. He seemed to take nothing seriously at all!

Davide was in fact more than a little in love with Cinzia. She was of course too old for him, a four year age gap being insurmountable to young teenage boys, but whenever he saw her he would run over and hug her. Occasionally she would walk down to the beach to see us all and it would be Davide that kept her talking into the night.

Then there was Diego Tedde. He was the fat one, the sensible one, the one with reason and intelligence. He seemed to know everything about Genoa's history. You only had to say "Ugo Foscolo"[6] and that would be

---

[6] Ugo Foscolo was an Italian patriot that fought in the Napoleonic wars. He lived in exile and was a poet.

enough to set him off talking about exile, battles, Genoa's forts and misplaced patriotism.

Diego's father had fought for the partisans in the war and was captured and imprisoned. Because he was a hairdresser he was able to survive the war cutting the hair of German soldiers in a prison camp in Poland. He was lucky, a number of Genoan partisans, all teenagers, were stood against the wall and shot right in front of Diego's house. His mother recalled how a German officer had put a pistol shot through the head of each of them as their bodies lie twitching on the floor. Diego's father, regarded as something of a local hero, was proud to say he knew them all!

Massimo Castanbrevia was the good looking one. His hair was reddish in colour and swept back. However, he always insisted that his hair was black, but as the summer wore on it simply became a deeper shade of red! This was often the butt of Davide's leg-pulling! He was calm in nature and really said very little. He had a cheeky smile and lived for the beach. Bocadasse was therefore his haven. Whenever he was out of sight of his parents he would light up an MS cigarette, purchased no doubt from a black market stall in the Caruggi, and lie back on the sand listening to the rest of us squabbling among ourselves, almost as though he were a mere observer.

Alfredo Creppi was the tough guy in the group. He hated the rich and seemed to pass his life with a chip on his shoulder. He had a quick temper and never backed out of a fight, in fact nothing pleased him more. His family had moved to the north from Sicily, as so many did looking for work, and only ever spoke in Sicilian dialect in the home. He was a compulsive user of foul language, and even made up words of his own. His favourite word was the often used a vulgar Sicilian word; "minchia". To Alfredo minchia was a verb, noun and adjective, no sentence was complete without it. He was also the expert at breaking wind-loudly, competing with Davide at times. Often he would do this in public just to embarrass us all. He held no fear and was always fighting over some triviality. However, despite his vulgarities, I was proud to call this course Sicilian my friend.

I was not really a Genoan. My family name is Citraro and my parents originated from a small village called Suni in Sardinia. We were therefore Sards[7]. Like many in that part of the world we came to Genoa before the war, on the daily ferry from Porto Torres, looking for work. We left our rural, almost backward, livelihood for the city in what was then fascist Italy. My father had worked as an industrial painter on the docks and then, influenced by a fascist parade organised by Marinetti, he volunteered and went to fight in Abyssinia. He told terrible stories about the war that portrayed a somewhat macho image. He spoke of gas warfare and dead children that were not the death or glory tales of an age gone-by. There was no comic book hero, just a true reflection on the horror of war! Yet he was really a happy-go-lucky,

---

[7] A person from Sardinia

gentle sort of man. His name was Pietro and my mother was called Silvia. They met in Sardinia and were always happy together. He could be strict though, and often clipped my ear for something or other. My mother's sister Rosa also lived nearby. She came to Genoa for work and met her husband Aldo working in the fish markets[8]. After they were married Aldo turned to drink and hardly ever seemed to be sober. He was a big man with greasy slicked back hair and a very long chin. I remember Aldo strolling home one night, his shirt unbuttoned to the waist and his jacket over his shoulder, hopping in and out of puddles, like Gene Kelly, and singing a totally incomprehensible song. Altogether we were outcasts from an agricultural past living in an alien industrial squalor. An innocent past tainted by a seedy present.

---

[8] Many Italians, especially in this period, travelled from the south of Italy to the north in search of work.

Chapter Three: The Outcast.

One late evening I recalled sitting around one of the overturned boats on the slipway leading to the beach at Bocadasse. It had been a really hot day, and now there was a cool breeze blowing in from the sea. Davide was telling jokes about the Carabinieri, popular at that time, in between smoking one of Massimo's endless supply of MS brand cigarettes. Massimo was laid back on the slope of the slipway while myself, Diego and Alfredo leaned against a white bottomed fishing boat.

Suddenly, and in his usual manner, Alfredo stood up and loudly shouted "Minchia, I have to take a piss". There was never anything gracious about Alfredo!

He walked toward the sea, emphasising his bow legs as he did so, behind the wall where no-one could see him in the shadows. It was Diego who noted how strange it was for one so course to not do it in the middle of the square!

"Perhaps there's hope for him yet - he has some sense of decency not to do it in public" he said with an air of sarcasm.

Massimo then came to his defence saying "you know he never swears in front of his mama!".

"I don't believe it" said Davide, "his pa used to swear all the time", "If you take minchia out of the language, Sicilians turn mute - we all know that!". Such philosophy was greeted with muted laughter.

As the sun was setting and we were preparing to go home Alfredo's voice rang out of the darkness...

"Minchia, Come here lads, you'll never believe this".

Eagerly we all walked down the slope to the water's edge. Alfredo was peering over the old sea wall and pointing. Slowly, unsure of what to expect, we all peeped one by one over the wall, our eyes level with the cobbles that made up the street before us.

On the other side of the road was a boy, about our age, playing with a wooden yo-yo. The strange thing was, he was dressed in a spotlessly white suit. He wore a cravat of silk and had the shiniest shoes you ever did see. His hair was covered in brylcream and parted roughly down the centre, just like Alfalfa[9]. He contrasted dramatically with our own ragged appearance. We wore a uniform of the poor that

---

[9] Alfalfa was a character from The Little Rascals seen on cinemas at that time

comprised of grey shorts and socks with holes in them, and a variety of dirty old shirts. The boy was standing in front of a house that, like him, shone like a new pin. The walls where recently painted in white and the shutters were the brightest green. In front of the house was a small boat on a trailer. It too was new and brightly coloured with a bright red bottom and a Royal Blue upper half, a golden stripe ran the length of the boat to separate the blue from the red.

The boy at first was oblivious to our presence, then, he looked over to a row of eyes peering over the sea wall. We all ducked out of sight immediately, as though he was something to be afraid of, then one by one we peered over the wall once again at the boy, who had now decided to look the other way.

"I know" said Alfredo with a half laugh "minchia what an opportunity".

We all stared at him wondering what sort of mischief he was up to now.

"This is our chance to get even with those rich bastards - they're not like us - they treat us like shit- come on" said Alfredo. I had nothing against this boy but he represented a ruling class and, at least at that time, I have to say that I resented everything he stood for!

We all followed like a row of toy soldiers towards the boy. One might ask where democracy ever came into it, but I suppose curiosity was our only motivation.

Alfredo asked the bewildered looking boy, who had now backed himself nearer to the wall, "who are you then - do you live here?".

The boy looked at as all one by one and said, with a rather upper class accent "no-I just come here in the summer - it's our summer house and my name is Luca - I come from Milan. Well now it's Milan, but I used to live in Brescia".

Davide asked what he did for fun and the answer was as boring as his dress sense.

"I read a lot and yes-my mother takes me to the cinema". For a second there was a noticeable silence as if his response had left us all in shock.

"That's not fun-you need mates-like us" said Alfredo with typical mischief in his voice. The rest of us clearly disagreed and shook our heads at the thought of it.

"Come on you lot- give him a chance- let him join us- he's OK" Alfredo's mischief was starting to show through his enthusiasm to befriend the now terrified Luca.

At the bottom of the street was an old disused boathouse that had once served as a den in our even younger days. Occasionally we sheltered there from the rain. After years of misuse the house was now a dirty and dangerous ruin. It was full of rats, many of them dead, killed by the greatest rat-catcher of them all- Ercole[10] the cat. The floor of the boathouse was full of dirt and paint, and in the corner was an old oil drum, still half full of diesel oil. This was to be the centre-piece of Alfredo's master plan, though we hadn't realised it as we all paraded down the street to show poor Luca a wonderful secret that only gang members were allowed to see!. Alfredo explained that such knowledge of the grand secret must never, under any circumstances, be conveyed to anyone. To this Luca nodded with enthusiastic approval.

Luca was starting to get a little worried, as he should have done. We had after all walked some distance from his house and into unknown territory.

"I must go back now" he said with a visible tremor as he spoke.

Davide now joined in the fun with confidence and clearly he had spoken in whispers with Alfredo, and was now well versed in the plan. "Come on Luca, you want to see our little secret don't you?-all the new gang members get to see it - but you must promise not to tell anyone - OK?"

Luca looked a little hesitant and stared at the floor as Davide spoke.

"Of course if you're scared we understand" said Davide with a mischievous grin on his face.

"No-of course I'm not scared" replied the boy with an unconvincing look about him! And one by one we

---

[10] Hercules

entered the boathouse, with the exception of Diego who whispered "I want no part of it - we'll get murdered if we touch him".

"You keep watch then fat-boy" said Davide.

"Stop calling me fat boy" said Diego with a grimace of anger written on his face.

"Well you are fat and you are a boy - well I think you are"

"Then I'll call you stupid then - because you definitely are!" Diego could certainly give as good as he got in a verbal exchange!

Outside the boathouse Diego looked around and for a moment his thoughts drifted to when he was a young boy playing in the sand with his mother. She had always molly coddled him and still did so. Suddenly he was startled by the racket and laughter coming from within the boathouse. Luca was screaming, Davide laughing his head off and there was shouting and cheering from the rest of us. Then the large blue doors burst open to reveal Luca, covered from head to foot in oil and dirt. The boys had dropped him into the drum and the oil ran down his face. He reminded us of the tar baby.

"I'll tell my pa, and then you'll see for this" cried Luca.

As he ran up the street, tears rolling down his cheeks as he screamed for help. I noticed a dead rat in his coat pocket, an obvious memento from Alfredo, which made me laugh all the more. I suppose that our upbringing in the Caruggi had hardened us to accept that this sort of behaviour was, to say the least, just good fun. Though I would condemn such actions today!

"Now you're one of us" shouted Davide as we all ran for our lives toward the square.

"You know" said Diego "that wasn't really on".

Davide put an arm around his shoulder and tweaked his cheek.

"I think you need a little oil too fat boy" he said and laughed with his familiar deep throaty laugh.

"Oh - well we'll have to find another beach now - because you have got shit for brains!" said Diego with a rare anger in his voice. He was right too. As we heard the commotion in the distance this had been a case of acting before you think. I for one would be afraid to return to that place.

For Davide and Alfredo it was a magical moment, but for the rest of us the responsibility that goes with maturity was, perhaps, starting to take hold. As we walked the long walk home I asked myself how soon we would dare ever to go back to Bocadasse.

Chapter Four:
Father Marco's Whiskey.

Father Marco was the strangest priest I ever knew, and as a good Catholic boy, I have known a few. He was an elderly man, of about seventy years of age. He was tall and slim with a few grey hairs brushed backwards over his head. He always had a smile on his face and yet he would hand out the most severe penance after confession. Once he even gave me the stations of the cross as a penance and it took me about an hour of prayer, followed by two days of aching knees and no reflection of the menial sins that I had committed.

Cinzia visited Father Marco regularly in those days. It was almost as if she was serving a lifelong penance for some undisclosed sin. She worked very hard and cooked his main meal for him. She was always available to work for Father Marco in daylight hours because she had an evening job in a bar somewhere in Nervi, a long bus ride from Vico Nievo. One annoying habit of the old priest was his constant whispering. It was as if he had a secret Godly message for each and every one of us. He would simply take your arm, lead you away a few paces from everyone else and whisper in your ear. Much of what he said could have been said in public anyway and served to confuse us all!

Behind the Church was a small garden. In the garden was long table with a set of benches on either side. It was both a sun trap and a pleasant shade from the wind. It was here Father Marco spent many hours reading good books and poetry. It was to this place I was once summoned for missing Mass and going off to play football with Davide. I remember the trepidation of walking from the Church and into the garden where the old priest, spectacles on the end of his nose, was reading the poetry of the great war poet Ungheretti.

Someone, and to this day I do know not who, had told him that we were seen leaving the church after only ten minutes, and then we were later spotted kicking a ball around in the square. It was unfortunately true, and how could we deny it to a priest? It wasn't as if we did it regularly, purely a momentary lapse of faith I suppose. We were wrong, and that was what we were going to say. Such rational would have made Diego proud of us, but now we were on our own.

"Ah!" said the priest on spotting us enter the garden, "keeping an appointment with the church! now that has to be a first in your case". A stern severity and sarcasm ran through every word!

He leaned forward and whispered "you may fool me, or even yourselves, but God sees all and you can't fool him" he said leaning back into his chair.

"So" he seemed to shout "what are we to do? I suppose an excuse is by now well prepared?". Father Marco clearly had wisdom on his side!

We really did not expect that one, perhaps this sort of thing had happened before.

"If I tell your mother Davide, what do you think she will do?" he said.

Davide replied with a very timid reaction "she would batter me Father".

The old priest sat back in his wooden chair for a moment, his hand on the side of his face and a frown running across his brow, giving our penance some considerable thought. Then, almost like the Seventh Cavalry coming to rescue the wagon train in some Roy Rogers movie, Cinzia opened the gate and said

"Signor Petroni to see you Father".

"Of course Cinzia, let him in- Ah good to see you Andrea!" said the priest, seemingly forgetting all about us completely.

Signor Petroni was a tall elegant looking gentleman of some renown. His moustache was so large it seemed to grow out of both his ears and his nose at the same time. Even on this hot day he wore a dark suit and a hat and looked decidedly uncomfortable.

"It appears that Signor Petroni's mother, an old lady in her 90s, has died and left a considerable amount of money to the Church" whispered Cinzia.

There is little wonder that Father Marco's thoughts were soon distracted. After all, such a donation was a clear guarantee of a place of Heaven!

Suddenly the Priest remembered his manners and decided to offer some refreshment to celebrate the Church's new found wealth.

"Boys" he said in his usual low tone of voice, "get me some of the good stuff from that cupboard over there".

For our lives we could never envisage a cupboard in a garden. However he did point to the clematis growing over the wall and so it was to there where we went. In the wall, slightly hidden by the creeper, was a small wooden door about two feet high. There was no lock and so we opened it. Inside, to our amazement, was about ten bottles of best Scotch Whisky. On a little shelf to one side were some small whisky glasses on the side of which was written "Scotland for Whisky". Could it be that Father Marco liked a tipple? Was he a connoisseur of Whisky?. Davide winked and we took the drinks over to the table.

"Cinzia, perhaps you could get some orange juice for the boys?" Asked Father Marco.

Dutifully Cinzia went back into the Church and returned with two glasses on a tray. Suddenly our purgation turned to celebration!

"Ah, there's nothing to beat real Scotch Whisky"

"Nothing at all Father" said Cinzia with a broad smile as she laid the glasses on the table in front of them both.

The two men talked and laughed about old times. They were clearly very close in their youth and their relationship was obviously more than priest and parishioner! Then they talked about the old lady who had died so suddenly, and naturally about the Church repairs her money would buy.

It all started to get a little boring as we sat there occasionally smiling, pouring a second glass of whisky, and observing without joining in any form of conversation. Then the Priest decided we had suffered enough and asked his guest if he could be excused for a moment while he bid us farewell!

With an arm about each of us the priest walked us briskly toward the gate.

"I think a penance is in order boys-don't you? I know how sorry you both must be!".

"I'll tell you what" he said "Now you know my little secret", referring to the whisky, "and I know yours".

Then he declared that his wish in life was to have a bottle of every kind of whisky ever made. "Now that would be something" he said.

"So" his voice now raised above a whisper, "tomorrow morning then, I'll provide the brushes and you two can clear up this garden. Now that's not too bad is it?".

"No Father Marco" was our feeble reply.

The fact is...... by his standards, it really wasn't too bad at all!

The following morning we arrived early to find two brooms waiting by the gate. The yard was a bed of leaves and litter. We set about our penance and after a couple of hard working hours; we had been purged of our sin! No one had ever asked if we were truly sorry but we were certainly relieved!

Chapter Five: 44c Vico Nievo.

There weren't that many places we could go. Our apartment was big enough for all of us, but Mama wanted to keep rooms for visitors, and therefore they were always spotless. That meant that the lounge was strictly out of bounds. My mother was very house proud and she was always spraying something or other around, the smell of which would often start me off sneezing. Most of our home-life revolved around the kitchen table. It was here we would talk and laugh and, depending where the mood took him, where my father would give advice and occasionally shout at us. He only ever hit me a couple of times and clearly mellowed as he grew older. If ever I got up in the night to go to the toilet he would shout out

"big queue eh son?"

and laugh his head off. However, if he had a bad day at work, it turned to "are you going to be there all damned night?".

He would often get up in the night and eat a piece of cheese in the kitchen. This was, I think, his real moment of peace from us all. There was always a large variety of cheeses in our kitchen. In many ways cheese was to him what whisky was to Father Marco!

The kitchen table filled the tiny room, and I never could understand how on Earth we ever got it in there. At meal times I had to crawl under the table to get to my chair. My father got pride of place, near to the window with the radio right next to his left ear. He always ate his food fast and Mama would shout "you should stop for a breath you know". This bolting of his food was often followed by a series of short belches and a fist pounding into his chest.

On Sunday we all went to Mass together, unless father was asked to work at the port which was a good enough excuse to miss it. The church of Santa Maria was close to Vico Nievo and from the outside had a dirty frontage hiding the glory within. The contrast was spectacular. The front of the church was covered in stucco plaster, a dim grey colour suited to a derelict port building. The surrounding buildings squeezed the little church out of view and was only really fully visible from the facing side of the square. Once you walked through those big old wooden doors it was like entering the Sistine Chapel itself; everything was golden coloured. Bright coloured statues and painted stations of the cross surrounded the congregation. The ceiling was blue coloured with small golden stars, like staring up into a winter sky.

Davide, like myself, was an altar boy in Santa Maria, which made his mother very proud, so much so that she would tell everyone that she met. However, my singing was so bad that I asked my mother not to send me to Father Marco's choir practice and she, having heard me on occasions, agreed. I even mimed during the service and left all those high notes to the other choirboys. Perhaps my absence from practice saved my mother from any further embarrassment.

Davide would always look over and wink in our direction and give a big grin to Cinzia, who always sat right at the front, and always looked bleary eyed on a Sunday morning because of her evening work. I recall once getting a real good hiding from Pa for laughing when Davide broke wind at the altar. He had clearly forgotten the acoustics in the Church were excellent. It came right at the end of "let us pray" which made it worse. The problem is that when you are not supposed to laugh, you laugh all the more, it's always the case. Through it all Davide kept a straight face, though afterwards Father Marco clipped his ear and told him to say the stations of cross as a penance!

Pa was an industrial painter. He worked on the docks and worked long hours. When he got home you could always smell paint and turpentine on him. He was always tired and would sleep straight after his meal. I recall him saying how well he was paid and how lucky we all were not to be really poor like

Davide. He had in fact accepted a contract to paint the inside of tubes and cylinders with some sort of anti-corrosive paint. When he came home his eyes would be streaming and he often had migraines. But the pay was so good he could never say no and dutifully worked longer hours for the money.

Sundays were days set aside for visiting relatives. Rosa, and her husband, a reputable drunkard, would turn up and sit in the lounge drinking coffee. Then we would eat the best meal of the week, in a really cramped kitchen, and talk about all things Sardinian. Often the war would come up in the conversation. My father had been called into Mussolini's Alpine force and served in the mountains until the Americans captured him. He told us once that they had fired one shell at the Americans and they had replied with about forty! He wasn't war-like and most of his war stories were funny ones. He would love to tell-and re-tell-a whole range of funny events. Like the time he saw a British patrol, which was under fire at the time, with an officer was wearing a top hat and carrying an umbrella! Or how some Sicilian call Ernesto became an expert in blowing up toilets in derelict buildings with hand grenades! Clearly his war was not all bad.

There was always sound in the house, even when we were not speaking. There was the wireless on the window ledge, occasionally hidden by the flapping net curtains. The valves seemed to last forever. It was a an old brown thing that really should have been thrown out, but it held a strange sentimental value for the family I suppose.

Cinzia's terrace was directly opposite, three floors up from the main entrance. She lived there with her mother. Her father had died many years earlier from cancer of the throat. I would often shout over to her with a hearty "ciao". It was worse when Davide came round. He would always make for the kitchen window and shout something like "anyone alive over there?". My parents thought the world of Davide and even gave him pride of place on the sofa, usually reserved for guests, in the lounge!

The most famous event to effect Vico Nievo was that during the war a shell, fired by the British fleet, totally destroyed the corner block of apartments. Now it was just derelict land, and another source of adventure for local children. On that same day a huge shell went straight through the roof of San Lorenzo Cathedral and miraculously never exploded. Everyone would call it an act of God, to this very day, the shell that was taller than me, stands in the entrance to the Cathedral.

Chapter Six: Cinzia.

If ever there was a woman with a secret it was Cinzia. Now, as she sits across this kitchen from me, the innocence of the woman and the victim that she became almost makes me weep. She was, to all who knew her, a kind young girl with a smile for everyone. She had a natural beauty that required no makeup. Her long dark hair, tainted with a red tinge, once flowed down her back and cascaded over her shoulders like a waterfall. Her eyes were big and undoubtedly radiated the goodness within. Her smile was broad and a permanent fixture of her beauty, enough to seduce any man. She was all things beautiful and yet so mysterious. I remember that she once gave Davide, her favourite among us all, a birthday card with the outline of a kiss which sealed the envelope with lipstick. He didn't sleep for a week. Yet, in reality, none of us really knew much about her. She discussed everything with us and yet told us nothing about herself. All we knew was that which was before our eyes every day.

One late evening we were sitting on the pavement in the street when Cinzia appeared. She was dressed up to say the least, yet she came over and sat down on the pavement between Alfredo and Davide. She looked a little upset and soon Davide asked her what the problem was. She told us that she hadn't been too well and left work early for a lie down.

"Will you lose money then Cinzia?" enquired Davide.

"No" she replied shaking her head,

"I can always make it up tomorrow".

We all looked at each other wondering what on Earth she meant by that, but she didn't explain.

"I'll have to go home and tell Mama I'm home tonight" she said with a look of trepidation.

Cinzia lived alone with her mother, yet her work at some bar in Nervi seemed to keep them both reasonably well. Their apartment was furnished with the best furniture and was always immaculate, not that we ever saw much of it. Occasionally Cinzia's mother would ask one of us to run an errand for her, mostly to the bakery, and that was the only time we ever saw the inside of Cinzia's home. We all knew she received no income from Father Marco. Cinzia's father had long since passed away and she was the bread-winner of the family. She seemed to thrive on the responsibility of it, unusual for a girl of around twenty. To all of us she had no boyfriends to speak of. There was one once who was so accident prone on his bicycle that everyone

Senso Unico

cleared the street when they saw him coming. Now and then she spoke of Saverio, a Sicilian boy at the bar in Nervi. None of us had ever seen him and we all wondered why she hadn't brought him home to meet her mother. Was she ashamed of him we wondered? After all in the late 1940s it was the done thing, and Cinzia was certainly a very beautiful young woman.

The fact is Cinzia looked troubled and it showed. Her brief chat with the gang was something of a relief for her. I suggested that she ought to go home and with some reluctance she said "you're right Tino" She slowly stood up and strolled over to her apartment door and we all started to talk about other things. Then, breaking the silent air like thunder, a rough angry shout rang out down the street "Cinzia!".

Out of the darkness, lit only by the dimmed gas lamp, stood a man resembling a Chicago gangster. He was about six foot tall, very broad, unshaven yet with black slicked back hair. He wore a dark expensive looking suit and very expensive shoes that shone in the reflection of the lamp.

The man marched towards Cinzia and took her by the arm. "Just what the Hell are you up to" he asked aggressively. Cinzia apologised and told him that she had to go home as she felt ill.

"That's not good enough Cinzia, I need my money, I pay the rent, how can I do that if you go home?".

Cinzia looked terrified and soon we were all on our feet to observe this strange event. I shouted to him, "leave her alone".

Davide took it further and walked closer to the man who was holding Cinzia's arm with a tight grip.

"Who the Hell are you?" asked Davide in a determined voice.

With that the man turned on him.

"Look son, you're out of your depth so go home".

The stranger then grabbed Cinzia's other arm and started to march her down the street. Davide, undeterred by the threat, followed them shouting

"Hey-leave her alone".

Suddenly the man turned and hit Davide full in the face. He fell to the floor and seemed motionless for a moment, rolling around uncontrollably. Whoever this man was he was violent and could hit really hard. I realised he was someone not to be messed me.

We all rushed over to help Davide to his feet and Diego looked shocked at the sight of so much blood pouring from his nose and onto his shirt. Davide was clearly semi-conscious to tell the truth, caught out by the sudden turn of violence, and therefore the fight had to be carried by his pals, and that meant us! I ran toward the man, now almost dragging Cinzia into the square. Alfredo and Diego followed in close pursuit. Then the man stopped again. He stared straight at us, reached into his pocket and pulled out the longest switch blade you ever did see. "Would you like some more?" said the man with a grin.

Then Cinzia said "boys, please, forget it, I will be all right".

Slowly we began to back away as Cinzia and the stranger vanished into the night, the echoes of their feet stumbling occasionally on the old cobbles and fading into some distant nightmare.

Davide began to shake his head and tried to recover his senses.

"Oh look at my shirt, my mama will kill me" was the first thing he said.

"God that looks bad" I said.

Diego, clear thinking as usual had the solution.

"Look Davide" he said reassuringly, "tell your mama that I accidentally head-butted you".

To that Davide looked aghast and proclaimed a better idea

"Listen Diego, that's ridiculous, if ever you head-butted me you would be dead now-let's say it was Alfredo".

Our thoughts then turned to Cinzia. We all sat on the pavement with the exception of Davide who chose to lie down with his blood soaked hands across his face. There was so much that we needed to know. Who was this man and what on Earth was Cinzia doing with him? Why did he hold so much power over her? Was he the Saverio she had spoken of so often? Cinzia, sweet innocent loving Cinzia, surely she couldn't be involved with such a violent man? She was afraid, on that point we all agreed. We knew that the bar she worked in was in Nervi, but none of us knew where. One thing we all agreed on that night was that we would be there for Cinzia and not run from the fearful stranger. If Cinzia wanted our help to get rid of him, then she would get it, no question.

As we sat around consoling Davide, who was now convinced that his nose had to be broken, we all swore to help our friend - Cinzia.

As we walked off down the road towards Davide's apartment we must have resembled a defeated army. We were silent now. Diego looked as white as a sheet and waddled along several paces behind. Alfredo had a growl on his face and in truth, as he was the best fighter among us all, perhaps he would have tackled the stranger better than poor Davide. Davide's shirt was now soaked in blood as he left us. As he turned to enter his apartment I noticed that a bruise was already starting to show under his eyes. He shed no tears and simply nodded with a half smile, then he closed the door. In later conversations I discovered that none of us slept that night, thinking and worrying about the fate of our dear friend Cinzia.

Chapter Seven:
A New Day Dawns.

I recall staring out of my room that morning and watching the sun rise. It was the dawning of a beautiful summer's day. The red rays of the sun coloured the white - washed buildings leaving only the deep green shuttered windows looking as they always did! I stared straight into Cinzia's kitchen, but there was no sign of life at all. Occasionally there was the bustle of workmen going about their business in the street and the shopkeepers started to open their shops accompanied by the usual wall of noise from the street below. I watched an old gentleman wander down the road and walk into a small cafe bar on the corner of the street. He had done this every day for as long as I can remember. Then I began to wander if I too would end up like him. Perhaps, I thought to myself, Davide's dream of going to America wouldn't be a bad thing at all.

Suddenly, and despite the glare of the hot summer sun, I noticed a light go on in Cinzia's kitchen. There she was, going about her day as if nothing had happened. No, her head must be as full as mine I thought. Slowly she moved across the room and began to pour what appeared to be a cappuccino. Then she seemed to stare up to the ceiling. As she turned I noted what appeared to be a dark area under her eyes. I couldn't be sure but Cinzia looked to have a black eye. The first thing I thought of was what excuse would she give her mama? There was a lot of explaining to do and for some reason I just had to be the one to speak to her.

After several minutes Cinzia appeared at the window. I caught her eye and she looked away quickly as if I wasn't there. Cinzia did see me though, I was sure of that, and I would go to her house if I had to. Then I leaned forward and shouted her name "Cinzia!". She returned to the window and looked at me with a vacant expression. "I have to see you Cinzia" I shouted. "All right" she replied. "I will see you in the cafe bar" pointing to the corner as she spoke," in fifteen minutes, and please, don't bring Davide". With that her mother appeared and looked shocked at Cinzia's eye. Clearly Cinzia was now offering some excuse or other as her mother walked away with her hands in the air and shaking her head!.

I couldn't wait to get to cafe bar and I arrived long before Cinzia turned up. I even forgot to bring any money and had to wait at a table without drinking anything. Then Cinzia arrived. She entered the bar with her head down to hide her face and sat opposite me. For all the things I wanted to ask her, I suddenly became speechless. Then after a short pause she spoke first. "I know there is so much you need to know about last night Tino, but I have so little I can tell you" she said. Cinzia then spoke of her situation as something she had got herself into and something she would get herself out of! "Just look at yourself" I told her. "Two black eyes and you're as pale as a ghost". She turned away for a moment and then she asked how Davide was. Before I could reply she interrupted. "You know" said Cinzia, "that boy means so much to me, I didn't mean him to get hurt".

Then she repeated her original question "How is my Davide?"

"Well" I replied with a pause for thought "he looks very much like you right now!".

Her big dark eyes opened all the more wider and she sighed.

I told Cinzia that we all knew she was in some sort of trouble and that we were there for her. She reached across the table and held my hand. I think this was the first time I ever felt so really close to her. With a tear in her eye she asked me to forget what had happened. She assured me that it wouldn't happen again and, for now at least, that was good enough for me.

Then Cinzia stood up and for the first time the barman, Adolfo, noted her face.

"Get rid of him girl" he said, "believe me, it will only get worse".

Perhaps he was right. I had a terrible feeling that this was not the end and everything Cinzia had said, so full of secrecy, was only said to pacify my inner fears. I couldn't speak for Davide, but knowing him as a very close friend, this explanation would not be enough.

Cinzia then turned giving a short smile to Adolfo and quickly walked back into the street. Adolfo then strolled over to my table where I was staring into space.

"What has happened to her?" he enquired.

"Oh, it was some sort of accident Adolfo, don't worry" I replied.

Then, like Cinzia, I walked out into the street, without even having the courtesy to drink one of Adolfo's espressos that he had offered to me for free!

All that was left to do now was to find Davide and try to calm down the situation. I approached his apartment and noted his bedroom window open.

"Davi!" This being the nickname that I alone had given to him! I shouted several times and before long a bruised and battered face appeared at the window. "Romeo, Romeo" he called with his arms spread out.

Clearly his battered look did not affect his sense of humour.

"Come down here you clown" I said "We have to talk, I've seen Cinzia"

Davide looked serious for a moment and then said "Oh Cinzia, me and her boyfriend don't get on you know!".

This was Davide's typical response to any crisis; to treat it with humour yet inside I know things were very different!.

After a few minutes Davide appeared on the street and, with our hands in our pockets and kicking the odd stone, together we strolled toward the port. Davide, despite his brave face, was very withdrawn. I told him about my meeting with Cinzia and what she had said about her feelings for him. For a moment a smile appeared on his face and he explained how he wished he was a few years older, how he would make sure that no one would hurt her again. Clearly Cinzia's request for us to forget everything was not going to be the answer for Davide.

As we walked and talked I looked at the huge bruising under his eyes.

"Your nose" I enquired "it's not broken then?"

"Well" said Davide "the Benotti family are tough bread you know, especially when it comes to noses".

"Look Davi" I said "let's just go on as if nothing happened, I'm sure that when the time is right Cinzia will explain everything".

It was then that I made the mistake of telling him how Cinzia too was bruised around the face. "The bastard" said Davide "the bastard"!

For a while I thought I could hear his teeth grinding together as he stared up to the sky in bitter thought and helpless frustration that I too had felt that morning.

"How can anyone harm a woman like that?". He stared into my eyes looking for some sort of explanation that I simply could not offer!

Now, and for the first time in my life, I noted a tear run down his face. It was then that I realised that despite the difference in age, Davide loved her.

Chapter Eight:
Back to Bocadasse.

Just like when someone falls of a horse, the answer is to get back on again. Well that was how Diego put it when trying to explain that life must go on! For several weeks now, since the unfortunate episode with the rich kid, we hadn't frequented our favourite beach at Bocadasse. The answer to everything was surely a late swim in the black water and to forget, at least for now, Cinzia's trouble. So, almost planned like a commando raid, we would go down to the beach and, if we are chased again, well that would at least be another adventure for us to laugh about. Diego also pointed out how salt water was good for injuries, and that convinced Davide of the merits of a return and feel the healing qualities of the Ligurian sea!!

It had been about five days since anyone had actually seen Cinzia. Clearly she was avoiding us.

Normally she always came over to speak and laugh with us all in the street, but not anymore!

Davide still looked awful. His eyes were still puffed up and blackened. Although he never went to the hospital, he had surely cracked a bone or something. He was constantly holding his nose with both hands and appeared to rock it from side to side. "What on Earth are you doing?" I asked with some degree of aggravation at the sight. "Well" said Davide "I think the back of my nose is detached from my face?".

At that we all started to laugh. I suppose that it was possible, but Davide just seemed to have a way with words that made anything, no matter how bad, seem funny.

"No, seriously, I can feel my bone grating against my skull when I wiggle it about like this!" He said moving his nose from right to left.

"I hear it grating" I said with amazement.

"Told you so"

"That would drive me mad that would" I said with some degree of admiration.

As we approached the beach at Bocadasse we all hesitated to make sure the coast was clear. The little bay looked really beautiful, as it always does in the summer. On the far side of the bay was a small wooden kiosk, erected since our last visit, selling ice creams and drinks. The beach certainly had more sunbathers than normal. On the beach itself were two

Senso Unico

upturned boats, ideal hiding places that could easily shelter us from the gaze of little rich kids. There was no sign of the boy, so brutally drowned in oil by Alfredo.. In fact the house that affronted the beach looked deserted with no sign of the beautiful boat that stood outside on our last visit. We couldn't wait to get onto the sand and into that blue water.

Alfredo suggested that we approach the beach along the wall, which would easily hide us right up to the water's edge. Then we could all sprint to the cover of one of the boats. It was a very tense moment, but one by one we slowly edged our way down to the beach beneath the sea wall.

As we were close to the first boat, a bright red upturned fishing boat, Alfredo gave one final glance over the wall to make sure that all was clear.

"Now" he shouted, and we all ran to the far side of the boat. There, in a long row, we all sat back to look at the sea.

"America" said Davide with a sigh.

"What are you on about now" replied Diego, but I could answer for him. "It was his dream, to go to America and open up a Pizzeria. To get rich and come back to Genoa for holidays" This was Davide's dream of escaping, but the philosophy of Diego might prove to be a barrier.

"Davi, life for all of us is a one way street"_ said Diego through a frowned and prematurely wrinkled forehead. Diego went on to explain that we cannot dictate our lives. That as our parents grew older, we had to take care of them. That we would all get some sort of work next summer and our debts would ensure we took no risks of losing it. Before long, we too would be old, and our kids would do the same.

"It's a path we all must follow" he said "just look at our parents".

What he said did have a ring of truth about it, but I for sure knew that my destiny lie away from Genoa. It was only when I would finally leave Genoa that I realised how deeply engrained into my heart the city actually was! I had thought about going to Rome, the Eternal City, and what's more, I could easily get home from there to visit Mama!

After a while we soon realised that we were all lying in the shade. The sun was firmly behind us, but to lie in the sun, meant move to the other side of the boat and to face the rich kid's house, and that wasn't too clever.

"Like it or not", said Davide, "I'm going to get wet in the black water".

Slowly, like Davide, we all started to strip down to our shorts. Then Davide stood up. "Get down, that's too obvious" shouted Alfredo.

But Davide revealed what he called a "cunning plan".

"Have you ever seen a crab walk?" he enquired.

"Well" he asked again in response to the silence!

"Well, a crab walks sideways", said Diego.

"Right, what a clever man you are, a true philosopher" blurted Davide, clearly back to his best form. Then we were told to form a line, with our backs to the danger zone; the rich kid's house! On Davide's command, we all started walking sideways towards the water.

"Left, right, left right"

"Soldiers we are not" said Diego

"Idiots yes" I said, falling over Diego's feet.

"Black water here we come" shouted Davide.

His words were mostly drowned out by our laughter. Everyone on the beach, and there were several families enjoying a day at the seaside, thought we were all mad, but we did get to the water eventually.

When it came to swimming we had the same problem, and for Davide the solution was also the same. To avoid being seen by anyone in the rich kid's house, we simply kept our heads facing the other way! Now this might sound simple, but in practice it became rather difficult.

The first to give up on the idea was Alfredo, who simply said "to Hell with it" and carried on as normal. Perhaps this action became the root cause of our complacency, as we all started to carry on as though we were innocents having a day out on the beach.

After a long spell in the water we meandered up the beach towards our waiting towels, carefully laid out on the shady side of the boat. Alfredo and Davide walked in the normal fashion, whilst myself, Massimo and Diego chose to do the crab walk once again! When I think back, those walking like crabs were the most innocent, and those who couldn't care less, were the true guilty ones! However, we all made it to the shade of the boat and had time to relax for a while. Alfredo lit a cigarette and sat there resting with his elbows on his knees. I lie back on the red boat with Diego whilst Davide and Massimo laid out on their now soaking towels. Together we watched the sun setting and the slow exodus of sunbathers leave the beach, until finally we were almost the last to go.

I noticed some blood on my towel. Eagerly I looked about my body to see where it was coming from. I had a long cut under my foot. The first thing I thought of was starfish. Perhaps one had cut me? Most likely I had cut my foot on some debris beneath the black water. Sadly, this beautiful spot fell victim to the litter of tourists.

What happened next made the trip a memorable one. As we were in the process of dressing, and getting more and more complacent about meeting the rich kid, the door to the house suddenly swung open. Out into the road stepped the little rich boy, shining once more like a new pin and certainly looking better than on our last meeting. Davide, as if struck by some incredible lapse of memory, suddenly shouted out!

"Oh- Ciao- it's me-remember me!"

"Davi" said Diego in a whispered voice that hid his astonishment whilst tugging at his arm to get out of sight!.

For a moment it was as if time itself stood still. Davide with a huge smile on his face slowly looked about to see our faces with mouths wide open at what he had done. Alfredo uttered one word, and did so in a mixture of disbelief and admiration: "minchia!"

Even the little boy stood still for a moment, and must have been as shocked as we were, before bolting back into his house with a cry of "papa!, papa!".

There was no time to waste. Without taking even the time to tell Davide what we thought of him, we ran toward the square, dropping socks and towels as we ran. The door to the house opened once more and out ran two very athletic looking men. Alfredo tripped on a piece of wood and lost his shirt in the panic. We ran off the beach and over the old Romano Bridge, which could only allow you to pass single file! Somehow we made it to the other side to hear the pounding footsteps and obscenities raining down on us from the other side. We ran into the square and, under Alfredo's specific orders, dispersed into the side streets.

"you go left we'll go right"

"see you back home then" I shouted

"Don't be late!" he replied.

Diego, well out of breath for his size, looked like giving himself up, so I grabbed his arm and almost dragged him through the street. Somehow we had lost them and dressed ourselves outside of a butcher's shop. Where the others had gone I did not know, but at least myself and Diego would live to sunbathe again.

Why Davide had chosen to greet the boy was something he never really explained. It just seemed the fun thing to do and was typical of him. I recall that as we ran, the only one laughing was Davide. Danger and adventure were his passwords.

Chapter Nine:
An Illness Bravely Born.

In the following weeks we had all but forgotten the traumatic evening with Cinzia. Occasionally we had seen her leaving for work and she waved sometimes, but never again did she ever come over and sit on the footpath for a chat. It was as if she had chosen to stay with Saverio, if that was his name, and ignore us. In short, she was different. Only Davide, now looking much better after his ordeal, questioned her motives for working in the bar.

"There are jobs, shift work though, at Italsida[11] if she needs money that badly" was all he would say.

"it pays well too, shift work though, but the pays good!"

Davide, more than any of us, missed our little chats with Cinzia. She stayed away from us for a reason, and

---

[11] A factory on the outskirts of Genoa

the thought of it ate away at Davide. Whenever Cinzia was mentioned his personality seemed to change. He became depressive and argumentative. I thought to myself, how marvellous it would be now, if only we had never met her friend Saverio!

This period also gave us great concern for my father Pietro. He had always provided us with a reasonably good life. This was due to the long hours spent working at the Genoa dockyards. For some months now he had done contracting work as a painter. We knew the work was bad, as he often came home with sore eyes and a runny nose. But the pay was good for the time and provided the family with good food and decent clothes. Little did any of us realise how my father was sacrificing his health to keep us that way!

He was a small man of about five foot tall with dark wavy hair, receding slightly at the front. He always looked unshaven and had very dark Sardinian features. Sometimes he grew a little moustache which made him look like a miniature Errol Flynn. He was a tough man though and could hold his own with anyone. In his Army days, having joined the Alpini as young man, he was a boxer, always fighting with someone, and his body was firm and muscular. The strangest part of his anatomy were without doubt his legs. They seemed shorter than they should be and were incredibly muscular and hairy!

On many occasions he got home late in the evening, and sometimes he would go and play at billiards in the bar. He didn't drink a lot, but he would sleep more than most. Basically he was exhausted all the time, and that also made him irritable. Sadly, I look back now and hardly remember him at all. He was a stranger to us because he lived to work, instead of working to live. If overtime was offered he took it – always! Of course we needed money, like everyone else, but I can never remember my father ever coming to the beach, or sitting in the square or getting drunk. He just seemed to work all the time.

I recall one late summer evening I was leaning on the wall by the bar, laughing and talking with Davide. Unfortunately Alfredo's favourite word "minchia[12]" had started to rub off on me. As Davide told one of his many funny stories I replied "minchia" only to feel my father's hand whack me right across the ear. I had no idea that he was walking past us. "Don't let me hear you say that again" he said, and walked off home in his paint covered dark blue overalls.

I went home a little nervous that night. He appeared different somehow. He was certainly more grumpy than usual, and something was troubling him. When I entered the kitchen he was listening to the radio and I noticed what looked like a spot of blood on the collar of his old work-shirt.

"Have you cut yourself?" I asked.

He replied with a groan and said "Oh that's nothing"

---

[12] Lit: fuck in Sicilian dialect

and then, as if feeling uncomfortable with my question, walked into the living room and sat on the sofa. Mother looked at me too as if I had said something wrong. She gave me one of her disgusted looks, though I really couldn't understand why.

After about an hour or so I started thinking about it all the more, and confronted my mother.

"What did I say that was so wrong Ma?" I asked.

Once again she looked worried about the question.

"Well son, it's like this" she said.

Then she told me that for some time now my father had been coughing up blood. The problem had started when he accepted a contract painting the inside of tubes with some sort of chemical paint. He had told my mother that he had felt much better working with a handkerchief around his mouth, though clearly his health was suffering because of his job.

"I'm sure it will pass when the contract ends" she told me, though I had this deep fear inside of me that he would only get worse.

It was at this time that we were beginning to shed some light on the double life of Cinzia, and my father had something to do with it. One evening he asked if I ever saw Cinzia, and I had to tell him that her boyfriend was a bit strange, and for this reason, we stayed away from her.

"I'll bet Davi is not too happy with that" he said with a little grin on his face.

"Maybe it's the company she keeps at the Gatto Morto[13]!".

With that I stood up as if someone had told me that war had just been declared! The Gatto Morto was the most notorious bar on Genoa's sea front. It was the haunt of prostitutes, Mafia, smugglers and anything sinister you could think of. They said that you could get anything you wanted there, like black market goods, guns and whores, and Cinzia was not the sort to be found there!! My father told me that on a number of occasions he had seen Cinzia going into the bar with a big well dressed man that sounded all too much like our friend Saverio. He said that she didn't stay long, because once, while he was chatting with a workmate, she left with another girl after a few minutes heading toward the old port!

"I didn't really want to say anything - but Cinzia has to be a prostitute – that is where she gets the money for that apartment, the clothes, well it makes sense!"

He uttered his words with a hesitant quiet voice and he knew, by the expression on my face, of the shock waves that were now running through my body. Cinzia didn't even look like a prostitute. She certainly didn't dress like one either, although I was never an expert on such things!. I had never heard her swear and to all she was a totally respectable young woman.

---

[13] Dead Cat

Then I started to doubt my father and said with some passion

"No Pa-there is an explanation for this-and I'll find out what it is".

With that my father sat back into his chair. I hadn't noticed that while talking to me he had leaned closer and closer toward me, as one does when revealing a deep dark secret. Then he closed his eyes and sighed saying "I do hope you're right son, I really hope you're right!".

All I could think of was to tell the others. Before my father had chance to snore I was out of the door and down the stairs, and on my way to see Davide. As I rushed into the street I ran straight into Father Marco. "And where are you going in such a rush?" he asked. Before I had time to say anything he had my arm saying "Look could you help me store some books, I can't get up those steps like I used to you know. Off course you can Tino, well done boy" and we were off. My timing was always bad.

It was the following day that I finally got to speak with the gang. As I told them what my father had said they looked at me as if I was going to tell a joke. It was Alfredo who spoke first and what he said shook us all. "I knew it, she's a whore. That explains it for me". With that Davide jumped on Alfredo with fists flying shouting "not true - you bastard", and the two of them rolled down the slope of the street. It took all of us to get them apart and in the confusion even Diego was punched in the ear! Two ladies from the apartments above opened their shutters and shouted at us to keep the noise down. Alfredo, speaking through gritted teeth, said that he had enough of what he called "this Cinzia business" and "until Davide grew up", he was through with him. Although we tried to reason with them both, they each headed off in opposite directions, their anger getting the better of them, leaving myself, Diego and Massimo, to sit on the kerb side with our heads in our hands. It was Diego who pointed out that despite all the rows we had between us, we had never come to blows, or fallen out, or even had to take sides in a dispute. I realised then how important their friendship was to me. We were more like brothers than friends and we had, after all, grown up together. Then an idea came to me about how we might find the truth!

Chapter Ten: Saverio Returns.

It was a very solemn looking Davide that I saw the following day. He was sitting down by the dockyard throwing stones into the water and watching the ripples make ever fading circles on the calm, yet murky, water. His head was bowed and each throw had an angry flick as the stone left his hand.

Slowly I sat myself at Davide's side. He glanced sideways for a second and sort of grunted as he threw the next stone. "Wish I hadn't hit Alfredo" he said giving me another sideways glance. My reply was instant, "I bet Alfredo wishes he hadn't said what he did". Perhaps in some way I actually did take Davide's side. Alfredo was in truth a rough kid, always looking for a fight, always saying what he shouldn't. And besides, poor Davide had suffered enough, physically and mentally, worrying about Cinzia.

I put my arm on Davide's shoulder, to offer some sort of comfort, and told him of exactly what I thought should be done. In truth, I had to tell Davide, though not with same gusto as Alfredo, that there might be some truth in what Alfredo had said. I did this with all the diplomacy I could muster and together we walked off together around the old port.

With the noise and the bustle of the Genoa dockyard ringing in our ears, with the sight of the ferry boats readying themselves for the voyage to Sardinia, I told Davide of my plan. We simply had to find out the truth and, if it was true that she was leading a double life, we had to at least try to get her to stop. My plan required going down to the dockyard at night. That would not be easy because none of us were allowed out so late. We would all tell our parents that we were staying at each other's house. What we really needed was an adult to vouch for us, but that wouldn't be easy. All we had to do was to follow Cinzia, and if needs must, confront her! The operation would be fraught with danger. We might have to confront the violence of Saverio again. We might even have trouble with drunken seamen or gangs. Genoa's sea-front was not the place for young boys after midnight!

After much deliberation, Davide, after much persuading, agreed to the plan. He also agreed to meeting Alfredo and letting our mission resolve the issue once and for all. Davide's concern went one step further too. He said that if all else failed, we should ask Father Marco to help. Even if that meant that Cinzia would never forgive us. I had no choice but to agree.

With the light fading fast we returned to Vico Nievo, satisfied that we would win our little war with Saverio. As we turned into the street, there, standing under the old lamp was the Devil himself, Saverio. We stopped dead in our tracks. No words were needed, he was waiting right outside of Cinzia's apartment. "Do you think it's all in the open now?" asked Davide. All I could do was to shrug my shoulders in disbelief. This man Saverio had no fear of showing his face where it wasn't welcome, and his stare was enough to freeze you dead.

We walked closer toward him and leaned against an old grey and battered wall. He kept his eyes on us both and we looked over to him. Davide gritted his teeth, clearly thinking about the beating he had taken on their last encounter. Saverio, whether feeling uncomfortable or not I really cannot say, slowly walked over toward us. "I wish I had a baseball bat" whispered Davide as we both waited to confront the beast again.

Then he spoke. "Cinzia works for me boys" he said. "More than that, she is mine, I own her". All the time his eyes stared into our frightened faces. It was the first time I had a chance to really get a look at him. He was uglier than I had imagined, yet very well dressed. I don't think I could even afford the handkerchief in his suit pocket. "Are you going somewhere?" I asked, almost as if it was polite conversation. Perhaps it was the fear within me that was rising to the surface. Suddenly he grabbed me by

Senso Unico

the throat and almost spat his words at me: "And is that any of your business - do you want a nose like your friend here?"

At that point my father walked around the corner. He was tired and dirty as always, and even coughing as he walked around the corner. When he saw this stranger with his fist in his own son's face, he suddenly came to life. "Oi- get your hands off my son!" he shouted, and couldn't get down the street quick enough. Saverio almost threw me against the wall and turned to face him. "Careful Dad" I said "he's not normal this one". I think, looking back, that I was more intent on insulting Saverio than defending my father.

What happened next seemed to happen in slow motion and totally unreal. My heart was racing and the words that I tried to speak just seemed to freeze there in my mouth. Saverio, almost casually, lifted a large ring on the finger of his right hand, to sit proudly on the knuckle. As soon as my father was within striking distance, Saverio hit him square in the eye. My father was badly cut above his left eye and the blood quickly flowed down over his overalls. From this point onwards he was effectively blind in one eye. Only now did I realise the courage of the man. His wound deterred him non. Before Saverio could celebrate the defeat of another of his victims, my father hit him in the mouth and Saverio rocked backwards against the wall. My father took up a sort of Gentleman Jim type pose, an obvious stance from his days as a boxer, and he seemed to hit Saverio at will. All that all that Saverio could do was to lunge back at my father and miss with every effort. Each lunge also met with a firm right hander and soon it was Saverio that was covered in blood emanating from nose and mouth!

Then I remembered that Saverio carried a knife and that made me all the more determined to protect my father. Together with Davide we waded into the fight. Now Saverio was getting a good beating from all of us and he retreated, staggering toward the square. Davide shouted "If you come back I'll kill you - you bastard" clearly relishing his revenge and the hatred for the man etched across his face. Saverio got the message and without a word ran off into the night staggering into walls as he left.

Our immediate concern was now with my father, covered in blood from the gaping wound above his left eye. Only then did we notice the crowd that had gathered in the street. Someone, though I can't recall who, gave him a towel to put over his cut. "You were great Pa" I said, only now realising that in his boxing days, he must have been awesome!

With our arms around each other we entered the apartment. There now seemed to be closeness between us that had not been evident in recent years! For once my mother had no concern for the blood that was now dripping onto her freshly polished marble floor. We stumbled into the kitchen and my father was soon cupping water into his hands and pouring it over his head. "I'm not as young as I used to be son" were his forlorn words to me. Davide sat silently on the kitchen stool and now looked as white as a sheet. Then he said, "someone has to do something about that man". My father turned and stared at him. "I know that kind of man Davi! and take it from me, keep out of his way, he's the Devil and he only mixes with sinners!!". Davide said nothing and just bowed his head and stared once more at the floor.

My father's advice didn't stop there. He told us forcefully that although we had known Cinzia all of our lives, although she was like a sister to us, despite her ventures to help Father Marco, which now seemed almost like a penance for her sins, Cinzia was really to blame! Davide raised his head at that and for a moment looked like he was going to say something, then he changed his mind and bowed his head once more.

I walked over to the kitchen window and stared down into the street. Onlookers were still gathered talking on the corner, under the lamp and outside of the old cafe bar. Then I noticed the door to Cinzia's apartment block slowly open. Cinzia looked out into the street and looked conscious of all the eyes that were looking back at her. Although no-one knew her secret she hurried off down the road with her head bowed in shame like one of those females that had collaborated with the Germans in the last war! I looked back at Davide standing next to my father now and offering a consoling arm around his shoulder. He was still leaning over the kitchen sink with the blood still dripping from his head. For some reason he chose not to go to the San Martino Hospital, but chose instead to bandage his head and wait. I said nothing of seeing Cinzia's hurried exit, but one glance from Davide told me that our plan would still go ahead!

Chapter Eleven:
The Dead Cat Mission.

Today Italy has sold its soul to the motor car, or so it seems to one as old as I am. If you approach Genoa from the sea, San Georgio[14], where Marco Polo was once imprisoned, is blocked from view by an autostrada[15] that snakes its way across the face of the old city. It's a shame really and I feel saddened by the loss of old things, but then again, maybe all old folk feel the same. After the war it was the bicycle that filled the streets leading from the old port, especially at the end of a shift. It was like the start of some great bicycle race. I remember once seeing a weak looking bespectacled man cycling for his life ahead of the chasing pack. He almost stood up on his bicycle as it rocked from side to side as he raced out of the main gate, determined to beat the chasing pack! Unfortunately, the entrance had a huge block of wood

---

[14] Saint George
[15] Motorway/ Freeway

where the gates neatly met in the middle. It was all that stood between the rider and glory! Unfortunately he hit the block at full speed and did the most perfect of somersaults over his handlebars and he lie there crumpled beneath the buckled wheels of his bicycle.

The fallen racer, like so many others at this time, wore a flat cap. I recall him casually putting it on his head together with his broken spectacles, before turning round to see a wall of bicycles racing toward him at full speed. I remember the shock etched across his ashen face with eyes as wide as saucepans. Naturally what followed was pure mayhem. The wall turned swiftly into a mountain, and underneath of the metal carnage was the poor racer. I recall laughing out loud as each rider, unconcerned with the poor man's health, abused him with a torrent of words not found in the Italian or any other dictionary!

It was near this entrance where the Gatto Morto was situated in those days. And this was to be our midnight rendezvous.

As I lay in my bed I heard my father's muffled coughing from the room next door. I prayed that he was really asleep and would not wake, as he so often did, to find me going out of the door. It was different for Davide of course. His mother was as deaf as a post and I bet that he was already waiting on the corner of the street. I had prepared well though; I had covered myself but remained fully dressed. In the summer the evenings were always warm and sweaty, so I dressed in just a grey shirt and heavy trousers. Not quite an Alpino[16], but it would do.

It was time to act and the first obstacle was getting out of the apartment quietly. I tip-toed across the darkened room and, despite the creaking door of my room, I successfully manoeuvred across the living room to the main door. There I turned the key, which now seemed to be twice as heavy as it had been, as slowly as I could. My face was contorted and my tongue was tightly held between my teeth as the huge key finally opened the door with a loud clang! I stepped out and turned the key once more behind me. At this point I decided that any future midnight romps with Davide would require a window exit!

As I stepped out onto the street a shadowy figure was leaning against the wall outside of the bar. Needless to say it was my old friend Davide. As he stepped out into the light he gave a smile and said "I never doubted you for a minute". And soon we were on our way to the Dockside, to the seedier side of Genoan life. It was, in a sense, our voyage to the Inferno. I was Virgil and Davide was Dante. The Gatto Morto was the centre of Hell itself!

As we approached the dockside everything grew even darker. I could hear the sea now and distant the sound of drunken laughter making its way through the darkened air. I could smell the sea and the distinct aroma of rotting fish.

---

[16] An Italian Mountain Soldier

As we walked along the sea wall the drunken laughter and shouting grew all the more louder and I started to feel a little afraid. For re-assurance I looked at Davide and I noted his face had a stern and determined look about it. He showed no fear and walked boldly forward, striding with a firm and steady step.

Somewhat conveniently, there was a small half demolished wall facing the Gatto Morto, an ideal point for a stealthy observation. The floor was slippery in places and the smell had become much worse, but somehow or other, we managed to lie down and peer over the wall. There in front of us was that dreaded bar. It was without doubt the most notorious of them all. The laughter coming from within was easily recognisable as the laughing and shouting we had heard when approaching the dockside. The bar was full and the bright lights from within lit an area bathed in the darkened shroud of night. In that darkness stood the ladies of the night. Leaning against walls waiting for their custom. Two or three were in conversation with a group of fishermen that sounded, although in whispered tones, to be Russian.

After a short while the girls left and walked toward the Caruggi. "I reckon they do their business in an apartment somewhere" said Davide. As we sat there looking at the bar a groaning came from beneath a truck further down the road. Two or three old trucks were parked on a piece of bombed land just off the road. Our eyes had now become accustomed to the light and we could make out a couple making love ferociously underneath of the truck! We looked at each other in disbelief and Davide said "God forbid if that's my Cinzia". For a moment I started to doubt whether coming here was really a good idea at all. Then we agreed to get a closer look and together we crawled over to a pile of bricks for a much clearer view. The lady, if that is the correct term, was fully clothed with her skirt raised over her waist. The man, a huge fat man with a heavy beard, was on top and was also fully dressed. It was the first time I had ever seen such a thing though I knew what to expect. Thankfully the girl wasn't Cinzia. This one was much more robust than Cinzia and wasn't beautiful at all. "Perhaps", said Davide, "the rough looking ones go under the trucks and the nice ones go to an apartment. The price is more for that I'll bet". As if to serve some educational purpose we watched to the end. The show had been so good I almost applauded at the end, and together we returned to the wall.

We must have watched for a good hour with no sign of Cinzia. This was, I thought to myself, a bad idea. I had laid behind this smelly wall half the night for nothing. I wondered then if even my father had been mistaken. Maybe it wasn't Cinzia he saw, or was that wishful thinking. Either way we had to get back home and into bed before anyone realised we were missing.

As we strolled back toward Vico Nievo we were too tired to discuss our next move, yet through sleepy eyes and yawns, Davide hinted at the most obvious plan; we had to follow her. When we turned into the street I said something I regretted the moment I opened my mouth, and yet I learned more about the deep feeling Davide had for Cinzia.

"You know Davi" I said like a wise old man.

"if she is a whore she's not worth this effort".

Davide grabbed me by the throat and pushed me into the wall.

"She's no whore Tino" he said in a determined voice.

"She's in trouble, and that's all!".

"All right Davi, if you say so" I replied half choking and gritting my teeth.

"One day Tino, she will come to me. I will get older and she will be my girl".

I smiled at him and said once more "Whatever you say Davi". My doubts were betrayed by the frown on my brow and a shaking of my head.

Davide then released his vice like grip and once again I could breath in the night air.

Then we went our separate ways. As we both arrived at our doors we turned and glanced at each other. Davide nodded his head approvingly and with a smile said "Thank you Tino" before quietly closing the door behind him. I now had to be as stealthy entering the apartment as I was leaving and it felt good to lie on my bed once more!

Chapter Twelve: A Rather Normal Day Considering!

I was awoken early the next day long before I was ever ready. I needed sleep and made a feeble excuse that I felt sick in the hope of staying in bed a little longer. It did no good at all. My mother had errands that needed doing and I had to do them. I literally crawled out of bed and through red, watery eyes, I looked at my rapidly aging face through the bathroom mirror. I thought that if I couldn't fool my mother that I was ill now, what on Earth would I have to look like to be poorly! I dressed regardless and my mother, in a flustered sort of mood, gave me money to buy fish. That meant another trip to the dock, which was the last thing I ever wanted to do having spent half the night there!

The sun shone brighter than ever that morning and it hurt my eyes. It was so bright that I could hardly make out who was in the street. I looked up and noticed Davide's shuttered windows were closed.

"Lucky Devil" I muttered to myself as I walked off thinking about the dream world he must still be in and trying to stay in the shadiest part of the street.

I took the same route as the night before and within a few minutes I was looking at the little wall opposite the Gatto Morto Bar. There I noticed a sort of black oil that wasn't visible at night. "Oh no" I said to myself and hurriedly took off my shirt to look at the back of it. There was a long greasy stain running straight down the middle, as if I had used the oily surface to slide on. My trousers too were covered along one side. I knew this would be a right beating if I didn't get some good excuse, so I decided that I would say I fell on the greasy surface near the market.

I then walked over toward the Gatto Morto and looked inside. There was a long bar of old dark wood and several round tables and chairs. It was very dingy looking really and only one picture, a painting of Genoa harbour, hung on the wall. The barman was cleaning glasses and one man, large and fat, was sipping a coffee. I wondered whether or not he was the rolly polly figure we had seen under the truck as it looked very much like him. Apart from these two solitary figures the bar was quiet. It was different by day. A sort of Doctor Jekyll and Mr. Hyde among bars.

Further down the street the market was coming to life. My head was still pounding with every sound emanating from behind the wooden stalls. Even the smell of the fish made me nauseous and I now associated that smell with sexual depravity. What I needed was a sleep and it was Bocadasse that came to mind. With that beautiful thought in mind I eventually arrived at the market.

Each market stall was staggered up a street leading upwards from the port. The selection of seafood was incredible as it always was. There was Octopus and Squid, Mullet and Haddock. Sardines, on my particular list, were in abundance. All I had to do was look for the cheapest and buy two etti[17]. However, I decided that day to buy straight away, no matter what the price, and have done with it. I just had to get home.

A firm hand then grabbed my arm. It was Diego. Good old fat man himself, I thought, I wonder what advice he would give me about last night? As I told him all about our midnight meeting he sort of leaned on his hand and listened intently to every word. Then he shook his head from side to side disapprovingly. "No good will come of this Tino" he said. Diego's theory was a simple one. All we should do is stop Cinzia and talk to her. Tell her we know her little secret, even though we weren't so sure. Cinzia was after all a woman and an adult. I then began to realise that such a rational approach was one that only he could have devised.

"What about the proof?" I asked.

"Who cares" he said "it's all gone too far anyway".

---

[17] One etto is about three and a half ounces. (abbreviation of hectogram – ettogramo)

He was right. My father was scarred beneath his eye. Davide had been beaten. We had spent half a night lying in oil watching two very ugly people making love, and for what? Then it dawned on me. It wasn't all for Cinzia at all, at least not as far as we were concerned. It was for our pal Davide. He had changed and been deeply troubled by what was happening in Cinzia's life. To this Diego had another piece of advice; "Everybody thinks they love someone you know, but at Davi's age it is no more than infatuation, and it will pass". His words were that of an old man rather than a young man no older than me!

I wasn't so sure. I thought then, as I always have done, that Davide really did love her.

"What are you shopping for?" I asked.

"Sardines" replied Diego "the poor man's salmon".

We bought our sardines after fighting our way through the mass of shoppers standing around the stalls. Diego was good to shop with because everyone seemed to move aside for him. Then together we strolled back into the Caruggi.

As we approached the Gatto Morto I noted a young girl waiting outside. She looked worried and slightly bedraggled. Her small frame was covered with a loose fitting red floral dress and she leaned on the wall much the same as the girls from the night before. "Any girl" said Diego emphatically "that hangs around there, by day or night, is no good at all". Then I thought about Cinzia. She could have been that girl! "Why do they do it?" I said. But every story must be different I suppose and money has to be at the heart of it!

Suddenly a ship's horn rang out and startled us both and turned our deep conversation into boyish laughter, and then, as if the Devil himself had played a welcoming tune, Saverio stepped out into the sunlight. The girl looked frightened and started to fumble around in her purse. "Not here" said Saverio angrily whilst looking about to see who was looking. Instinctively we both jumped into a doorway and looked the other way, but we were close enough to hear. "Get in" he told the girl and dragged her arm, just as he had done with Cinzia. "There's your proof" said Diego, pointing out that she, meaning Cinzia, was in league with the Devil himself. "Saverio" he said "was Cinzia's pimp!"

We edged our way toward the bar and peered through the dirty open window. The girl was sitting at one of the tables where a coffee had been summoned. The barman was smiling at Saverio and shaking his head in disapproval. The girl had clearly done something wrong and was being scorned for it.

Saverio sat at the table drinking a beer. He leaned over toward the girl and once again she began to fumble through her purse. Then she handed him money, a handful of notes! Saverio counted out the notes on the table and shook his head. Then he smiled at her. It was an evil smile. Saverio was one of those people that never really smiled, and when he did, you wished he hadn't bothered. He then looked to be giving the girl advice. Diego pushed me aside for a better look.

"He's the pimp" he said

"and that young thing there, she's his whore".

"What" I said. "Where do you get all this?".

"Oh I read a lot" he said and together we walked away from the bar.

Although I wanted to stay, I followed Diego. It was like putting down a book before the final chapter had been read. I, like Davide, felt drawn to get involved and yet I was afraid. I was afraid of the man that Saverio so obviously was. He radiated an evil that is visible at only a short glance.

"You know what Diego" I said running to catch up with my overweight pal.

"I really would like to do damage to that evil bastard"

"Silly idea. Forget him. It's not worth it".

"Oh so if someone murders someone do you say forget it because they're bad?"

"No, but what the Hell has it got to do with us?"

For a while I stood and stared at Diego, shocked by his response. Probably it was just the mood he was in, but I wasn't happy and decided to let him know.

"Listen, next time some street scum comes along and smacks you in your fat face, I'll say, well that's life, nothing to do with me, OK?".

Diego looked remorseful about what he had said and my anger had made the point.

"Tino, this could be dangerous. She's old enough and stupid enough to make her own way. She might be a lovely looking woman.... Let me tell you Tino if I gave you a gift for Christmas, a box wrapped in bright blue wrapping paper with a big ribbon. You would say great!... right"

I looked at him and uttered a meek sounding "yes"

"Well what if you opened the box and found it full of shit?"

"what?"

"Yes- full of shit- would it be a great present then?"

"Of course not" I replied wondering what he was going on about.

"Well Tino" Diego moved closer "Cinzia is like that box. What's inside is not what you would imagine on the outside!"

I stood there for a moment and I have to say I smiled a little at his words of wisdom. I had never heard it put like that before.

"You have a way with words fat boy, you should be a psychologist or something like that".

Diego smiled and then he said "Davide wouldn't take it like that though. So don't tell him the same, OK?" His words of advice made sense to me.

I agreed and together we headed back into myriad of streets that made up the Caruggi.

Chapter Thirteen: Carlo's Cwetins!

Carlo Muro was a young boy revered throughout the Caruggi for his daring. He was a born troublemaker. Even by the strict standards of the day, he held no fear of punishment. In all things he would make a good Saverio, a Mafia boss, a pimp, a thief and a even a violent man. Yet he was also the subject of ridicule, at least behind his back, for he had a speech impediment. Carlo could never pronounce the letter "R". It was sad really because his name contained the letter R. When asked his name he would reply in a way that was certainly understandable, yet what came out was not a true sounding R. At some points it was more like a W!.

Carlo's fame had spread throughout the Caruggi after an act of unbelievable cruelty. An act that was despicable and yet had a funny side to it! Some months back Carlo, and his gang, had captured a stray wild cat. The poor thing was put into an old sack weighted down with a large chunk of concrete. Now Carlo had learned to play some coherent notes on the bugle. He had been taught by his grandfather who had spent his entire adult life in the army. The cat, which had accounted for a large slice of the rat population in the Caruggi, was ceremoniously thrown into the dock to the sound of the last post, played by the charming Carlo, whilst his band stood rigidly to attention, saluting as the poor old cat sank to the bottom of the sea.

Carlo clearly had a sick sense of humour and was not dissimilar in this respect to Davide. However, Carlo could be downright nasty too. Practically everyone was afraid of him and I forget how numerous were the occasions that our two gangs had fought. He only ever came into Vico Nievo when he was looking for trouble or bored.

He had five or six boys in his little band. Like all sheep they followed their shepherd everywhere. I really don't think any of them could even think for themselves. Davide called them Neanderthals[18]. There was however one name that really stuck; "cwetins"[19] The name came from the derogatory term "cretin" and was altered to suit way that Carlo might pronounce it!

---

[18] Uomini di neandertal (Italian)
[19] From the Italian "cretini" – which in Carlo's case would be pronounced "cwetini"?

It appears that Alfredo had called out this name to Carlo several times and this in itself was enough for war. However, Davide and Carlo had taken the joke one step further. They had purchased a postcard of old Genoa, depicting the sea front. The card gave Carlo a hint of where, or even who, it had come from!, The postcard's message was written using the letter "R" repeatedly throughout. Every word used had an R in it, and as I said before, even poor Carlo's name also had a dreaded "R" in it.

It wasn't really his fault. When he was born, how on Earth could his parents know he would never pronounce his own name properly? The card was sent and signed by a supposed "admirer", a word which Carlo could never get past his own lips. Alfredo and Davide had laughed themselves senseless playing out a scenario of Carlo reading his card out loud. Somehow, the news had found its way back to Carlo, such is the impossibility of Davide ever keeping anything to himself. Now it was war!

One day shortly afterwards, as we sat out in the midday heat, some of us kicking an old leather football around, two scraggy looking kids of Carlo's gang had showed up. They approached us slowly, but being just the two of them, it was clearly going to be a message from Carlo. They were very scruffy looking and one wore a flat cap and braces. His clothes were probably handed down from his older brother as was the way of the Caruggi. We must have looked the same to him!

"What do you Cwetins want?" barked Davide in a sarcastic tone of voice.

"Meet us at the old Roman Arch, no sticks. Carlo has a score to settle!"

"Oh - no sticks - are guns allowed?" Davide laughed off the request. Now Davide grabbed the cheek of one of the boys and said "Tell him we'll be there and I will look forward to beating the crap out of him! Now get out of here" giving the boy's face a push as he spoke his last words. "Tomorrow at seven and no weapons. Just make sure that stammering bastard turns up!"

The two turned and walked off down the street, looking backwards occasionally as they did so as though they wanted to do something but were too afraid to do it!

"What if we don't want to fight them?" asked Diego. "After all we've beat them before and what's the point".

Davide's answer was simple. "This time it could be the last time!" Next year who knows where we will be. This is the last battle boys, so let's make it a good one!"

Davide then pulled out from his trouser pocket a small scout's knife. He opened it up to reveal a very serious blade that looked like a Bowie knife. It could have been used for gutting fish!

"Now where the Hell did you get that?" I asked.

"Found it - near the Gatto Morto one night"

"And what will you do with it? And - what were you doing at that seedy place at night anyway?"

"I might just end that Bastard's career once and for all" As he spoke those words he stared out in an almost trance and sounding like he meant it.

Someone had to set a rule and that was down to me. "I think I can speak for us all here. If you bring that, you're on your own!" I said firmly.

Although I hadn't realised it at the time, Davide had clearly been in the vicinity of Genoa's most notorious bar, the famed Gatto Morto, on at least one night, after our earlier reconnaissance! It is true that you could easily get hold of a weapon on Genoa's sea port and I had little doubt that he had genuinely found it. After all he would never have paid for such a thing - and why?

The following evening we all made our way to the Roman Arch. It wasn't really a Roman Arch, just a huge destroyed building with a large door facing out towards Genoa's famous lighthouse. It was an ideal battle ground, lots of loose bricks lying around, piles of rubble and an impressive gateway that would have done the Coliseum proud. We were Gladiators about to face our enemy for the last time. This time there will be no mercy, just victors - and losers. The old ruined arch had been the scene of many past battles and held lasting memories for us all. Once Davide had a cut in his head open in a gang fight. The wound must have been at least three inches long! He was proud of those stitches and wore them like an old soldier wears his medals. Now the scar was hidden by a long wispy fringe that fell across his troubled brow, an outward symbol of the hidden turmoil within.

The only inhabitants of the arch were about fifteen or so stray cats. All colours and sizes, and none of them too friendly either. As we approached the arch their screams sounded like hundreds of dying babies which only added to the eerie atmosphere of the place.

"No Mercy" shouted Davide. He meant it too. In hindsight I know now just how ready he was for a fight. All the emotion of recent months were about to explode - right into Carlo's face!

As we approached the arch the stray cats scampered across the rubble, their homeland invaded, their privacy disturbed by an air of violence and the screams of tribal vendetta. The evening sun, fading fast now, cast long shadows across the debris and gave us all an indication of the army that stood before us. They formed a line, all serious, all staring, all ready for the battle to end all battles. There were about twelve of them, clearly outnumbering us, and some held short sticks, so much for the no weapons call! Some held stones and tossed them into the air. Juggling gangsters was all that came to mind.

"Come on!" yelled Davide with an angry scream that must have been heard right across the Genoan dockside. He marched out at a fast pace staring straight at Carlo. Nothing would stop him, not even the stones that narrowly missed his head as went straight for the main man. We followed of course and soon we were embroiled in the battle to end them all.

As Davide got close to Carlo his enemy seemed to back off, such was the determination on his face. Then he erupted with a string of punches into Carlo's face and body. Under the weight of it all Carlo was soon grounded and clutching his stomach. While this was going on several fights had broken out around them. Diego was swinging a huge piece of timber and smacking it over the backs of every Cwetin within rage, though more often than not he missed and hit the nearest crumbling wall!. We all fought well that day, and it was good to have Alfredo and Davide with us, but it was Davide that really brought things to a close. With Carlo lying half conscious on the floor, something that clearly deterred the other Cwetins, Davide started to kick his victim. Again and again his boot was buried into the prostrate Carlo and accompanied by a string of foul mouthed abuse. "You hair lipped bastard, fucking die" But the kicks rained in relentlessly and brought the whole battlefield to a halt. We all stared for none had ever seen anger like this before. I grabbed at Davi's arm and shouted into his face "enough!" and then in a softer tone "you'll kill him Davide". With that he stopped and looked into my face breathing heavily. He turned away and kicked a brick into his victim. "Right" he bawled turning to the remnants of Carlo's gang "leave now and never return. If I say any of you come back here you are dead!" And who would doubt his word.

Slowly Carlo's weary warriors helped their leader to his feet. He was spattered with blood and in a daze. They carried him off and they vanished, never again were they to be seen in the Carrugi. We all stood there in silence and then Alfredo looked at us with the broadest of grins. "Yeah!" He lead the way with his rebel yell and we all joined in. The sweet smell of victory was ours and day belonged to the noble army of Via Ippolito Nievo. Although I didn't realise it at the time, we had left more than our blood on that hallowed ground, we left our childhood there too!

Chapter Fourteen:
A Coming of Age

Saverio had not been seen on the street for months. Summer had turned to winter, winter to spring, and summer approached again. Our school days were over and we were about to embark on a world of work. The only problem was that work was scarce now. Things had become even worse since the end of the war, yet our beloved government kept saying that the situation was getting much better. How wrong they were! I was lucky really, I have always been lucky when it came to getting work. I cycled around the streets, and even the full length of Via Italia, pasting advertising posters to boards, walls, windows and wooden fences. I didn't know then but eventually I would make a lifetime career selling advertising! It didn't pay too much but it kept me busy and I was able to make a telling contribution to the family purse. At last I was a valued lodger and I started to take on the responsibilities associated with growing up. Davide, who had already started to lose his hair and looked much older than he was, was working earning black money, the kind that avoids the tax man and half the population seemed to be doing it. He worked in a small bar and coffee shop, just a stone throw from the bombed ruins of the Carlo Felice theatre. The ravages of war were still with us.

It is strange how unexpected events can change a life. It had been almost two years since the fight with Carlo and in that time illness had gripped my father and slowly turned him into something unrecognisable. Cancer was slowly eating him to the bone. He was a heavy smoker and it was, at least as we believed, that which was to be his killer. I was entering a period of my life that would burn itself into my troubled mind forever more.

I was paid a weekly wage and it came in cash tightly packed into a small brown envelope. Every week I had to sign for the packet and then ride home on my trusty bicycle to hand it over to my mother unopened. She then carefully checked the contents and gave me some pocket money, to which I said a very grateful thank you. At least I was paying my way!

My father's brother, Uncle Tobia, was a regular visitor and I was never really sure of him. He had great war stories that were often funny and had us all laughing and yet he had a serious side to him that seemed un-nerving. He was tall and slim with black hair swept straight back off his face, lathered in brylcream. He wore dark rimmed spectacles that sat on an overly large, and very crooked nose. His job as a warehouse manager in Sampiedarena, an important area in Genoa, was well paid and with no wife to keep, he lived life as a wealthy and contented soul. As my father's illness worsened in the coming months I was to see much more of Tobia.

My father had been spending a lot of time at the hospital of San Martino. He was having radium treatment for his illness but by March he clearly knew that the battle had been lost. On a number of occasions I had seen blood stained handkerchiefs in the washing basket. As I look back now I suppose I never accepted that he would die. Death has always had that strange effect on me. It still never seems real and only ever happens to someone else. Maybe that is the best way to live with it, not to trouble yourself with the worry and just get on with life. But dying he was and it was all to end so suddenly.

After one last short spell in hospital my poor father returned home looking a shadow of the man we once knew. He was very thin and hardly any hair. He coughed and had hardly enough strength to climb the stair. He spent most of his remaining days lying in his bed and drifted in and out of consciousness. I still can't remember the last words he ever said to me but I wish I could have told him that I loved him, before it was too late.

I remember those final hours as if it was yesterday. The room was dimly lit and my poor father was cradled in my mother's arms. His breathing was loud and broke the silence of the room with a haunting echo. Father Marco was there and looked at me with a saddened smile across his face. Before I arrived he had administered the last rights and prepared my mother for the inevitable. The doctor was there too. Doctor Cordara was a small plump man with a huge moustache that partly hid his mouth. He carried with him a smell that said "hospital" or maybe it was just my imagination.

The clock seemed to tick ever more loudly in rhythm with his laboured breathing. It was unreal as though time itself had stood still. I couldn't believe this was happening. How could God let this happen to good people? My head was filled with questioning and fear. Then, suddenly with one long drawn out breathe, the breathing stopped! My mother called his name and held his head closer to her. "He's gone now" said Doctor Cordara and quickly followed it with a sympathetic "no more suffering!" I felt a wave of energy sweep over my body and walked out of the room, I could stand no more. I walked through and into the kitchen and stared straight at the wall. For a moment I thought I heard a huge bell ringing in the distance. I still hear that bell today and I had never heard it before. Was this a signal, a farewell, the gates of Paradise opening for my dear father? I really couldn't explain it, but I am certain that I heard that bell.

Father Marco entered the room and told me that I should go to find my uncle. He would be in a small bar in Vico Gabrielle called Paolo's Bar. I was to find him and bring him straight away. I ran all the way. I remember running past the long red brick wall with arches, the red brick shone as the drizzle ran down them. It was a short distance really but it seemed as though I had ran a marathon! Then, standing before me was the Bar, like the windows of Vico Nievo it was a distinct shade of deep green. As I walked in the bar it was daunting to find that it was packed. I couldn't see Tobia anywhere, just large old men drinking, smoking and laughing. Then a voice called out "who do you want son?" "Tobia" I replied with a trembling voice. It fell silent as if the news had reached the bar before I had. "He's gone son, gone to see how his brother is. Are you Tino?" I didn't reply I just ran out and into the night. I ran and ran and never once noticed how tired I was. Soon I was once more in Vico Nievo. Before me, standing in the shadows, was Cinzia. She said nothing but held out her arms and cradled me. I cried like a baby and she held me tightly until I had stopped. "Anything I can do you just let me know" she said and I knew she meant every word. I cried and cried uncontrollably and she held me all the more the more tightly. It took me a while to compose myself, but somehow I did. Then I pulled away from her and looked toward the front door. I walked back into the house, back into the living room and Tobia was already sitting in the kitchen. He never spoke; I don't think he

Senso Unico

knew what to say. Our mutual stare spoke a thousand words and it was enough.

Near the entrance to Genoa's old cemetery is where my father was buried. As you enter the cemetery there are stalls selling flowers and a cramped area where it is almost impossible to park a car. In those bygone days the cars were never such a problem but the stall seemed to have always been there. There were two thoughts that stayed with me from this very sad time. My mother had insisted that we said our goodbyes together and with our arms around each other we looked over his open coffin as it rested there in the church. "Hold his hand" she said and this I did. It was cold and unreal and he looked like a marble statue. I kissed his forehead and it was like kissing stone. My father had gone, this just wasn't him, his spirit had left him. He was dressed in a long white robe with gold braid and his hands were down by his side. On his chest was an old wooden rosary and he lay on white silk. I recall little of the service, everything was but a blur, and the kind words that were spoken, but I remember every detail of how my father looked.

As the cars pulled out of Vico Nievo the street was packed. It seemed like the whole of Genoa had turned out to say goodbye. I saw Alfredo and Davide standing together. They both had an angry look on their faces and they nodded toward me as we slowly followed the coffin on foot. Then I saw Diego. he had been crying and was wiping a tear from his eye. Massimo placed an arm on his shoulder and gave me a little smile. Then I felt Cinzia's hand touch my shoulder and she walked behind the coffin with all of us. I recall that I had started to think of all those sooty looking marble statues in the Cemetery. I wondered whether or not one might be built to my father one day. When we arrived at Staglieno Cemetery the flower sellers were very busy. We drove past them and through the main gate. We turned to our right and close by was an area of land almost untouched. A line of trees ran along the roadside and I counted three trees in when the cars drew to a halt. I had to mark this place well so I counted the trees once more. I saw an old tap and a sink on the roadside. Then we walked three rows in. Now I could never forget where to go. As my father was laid to rest my mother gripped me tight and I heard her mutter "I will never see him again" and she started to weep. There was no shortage of comforters and Tobia was the first to do so. I didn't cry, it was the shock I suppose. I just stared into space, a head full of nothing at all.

Returning to Vico Nievo was different now. The street had emptied and was still. The house seemed to have an echo to it and an emptiness that I couldn't describe. I wondered if there would ever be laughter there again. I started thinking back to happier times. I remember when my father had a bowl of water on the floor and two lead soldiers. He told me that one was me and he was the other. Then he dropped them from a great height into the water to create a huge splash! And we argued over who was the best diver! Ridiculous now to look back at that. I walked into the kitchen and turned on the radio. Even the music was solemn. Suddenly there was a knock at the door. I opened it and there stood Cinzia. I stared for a second and then we all went into the kitchen where Cinzia made us all a cup of strong Italian coffee. I didn't mention recent events or Saverio as we sat there talking and reminiscing. But it was comforting to me then, as it is now, to sit before that beautiful smile. At least I was home again.

Chapter Fifteen: Tobia

Tobia was my father's brother and I respected him as one respects an uncle. His jet black hair, the most striking feature of the man, was made all the more shiny through an over-use of brylcream. He was a joker and loved to talk about silly war stories that featured in his long military career in the Navy. He had a charmed life in the armed forces before he left to work in a warehouse opposite the old port. I suppose he was our most regular visitor after the death of my father. I was naive in those days and I hadn't ever noticed that, as he was not married, he might one day replace my father! But that is exactly what he did. However, at first I found the relationship between my mother and Tobia awkward and difficult to accept, but their closeness came home to me about two years after my father had died.

At that time I had found employment pasting posters around the city centre. For this job I needed a trusty old bike and a lot of energy. The pay was poor but I had a degree of freedom and there was no-one watching over me every day. Each morning I cycled to work, a short distance of only ten minutes or so, and I reported to an old terraced property in the heart of the Caruggi. It was basically a church like entrance with dark grey stone walls filled and two huge old wooden doors. The street outside always smelled of urine and was full of stray cats. I would go in and collect my posters and carry them in a large canvas bag. After a few months they even gave me a blue overall which actually fitted! I looked the part and cycled around the town doing my job to the best of my ability. My mother always kept more than half of my wages and, though it seems unlikely looking back, we managed to survive.

One evening I recall lying on my bed staring at the ceiling. I was looking at a long crack that meandered its way from the wall to the centre light bulb that seemed to be supported by a long, poorly made, cobweb. I imagined it to be a river on a map. For some strange reason I thought of the River Darling in Australia, just because Massimo had once told me how his dream was to paddle a canoe the full length it for some reason that he never really explained! The room was quiet and, after such a long day working in the midsummer heat, I was very weary and started to fall to sleep. Then I was awoken by a noise. It appeared to be a moaning noise and I soon sat upright on my bed to listen. I quietly walked across my room and I noted that the noise was coming from my mother's bedroom. The door was not closed properly and I was able to look through the small opening. I stepped back in disbelief at the sight before me. Tobia was in my mother's bed. Unsure of how to react I returned to my room and sat on the bed again, this time my mind full of thought and anger within. I see it very differently now but at that time no-one could replace my father and I was disgusted at both of them. From that moment on I was always cold with my relationship towards Tobia. No matter how he joked I could not find it within me to even smile. No-one ever questioned me about my reasons but our relationship deteriorated, even after my mother married him just twelve months later.

On occasion I took the opportunity to argue with him. Our worst row occurred when he told me to "put your shoes away!" I soon responded aggressively telling him I was no longer a child. And then he said some words that stayed with me for a long time. he said "in this house you are no more than a lodger - remember that!" Those words really hurt and our relationship appeared to be damaged forever. My answer was to walk out, storm past my mother who was pleading for us stop arguing, slamming the door as hard as I could, and I walked off into the night air of the Caruggi. I walked and I walked toward the docks, towards the night clubs and bars that had become more numerous with the end of the war.

With the bright red lights beaming out towards the grime and filth that was the dockside, I noticed the shadow of someone familiar sitting on a crumbled stone wall. It was Davide and at last I had someone to spill my troubles to. Although, he too looked somewhat down, and offered me a slight smile as I sat beside him. "Now then, long time since I saw that miserable face" I said as I sat beside him feeling some of the anger lift from within me. He didn't answer and just gave a short laugh. I asked him why he was sat out there staring at the city like that. He looked at me and then, with a nod of his head, he gestured towards the Gatto Morto bar. I looked at him again and then I realised. "You're not still following Cinzia are you?" I said with amazement "after all these years?" He moved off his stony seat and sat on the floor resting his back on the wall and staring up to the night sky. "I know" he said "better off looking for shooting stars! Do you know that tonight we are supposed to see hundreds of them?" So I joined him and sure enough we spotted a long silvery trail fly across the night sky.

Davide told me that he was now working in a bar doing black work[20]. He was now employed in a corner bar near to the Carlo Felice theatre, or at least what was left of it after a bombing raid in the war. He was depressed with his life and told me that he had an uncle in Baltimore and he was thinking of leaving to work for him. "Why don't you come?" he asked. In truth it did seem exciting, but I was Genoese and thoughts of leaving had vanished with my childhood. Finally he answered the question about Cinzia. "I love

---

[20] Cash payment without paying tax. What is called in England "a backhander".

her you know" he said and I was almost tempted to ask who! It had been some time that we were watching the stars and I had almost forgotten. "Listen" I turned toward him "you will never win the love of a woman like that, besides she's older than you are". At this point I had, for the time being, forgotten my argument with Tobia and our thoughts were once again dominated by the past.

As I, sitting in that room today, recalled my encounter with Davide to Cinzia, she squeezed my hand all the tighter and smiled at me. I told her that I should be going but she sat me firmly down into my seat. "No Tino, I would like you to stay a while. I need to know more!" And so I sat my aging frame back into the chair and so I continued with my story.

Chapter Sixteen:
A Night to Remember

As I sat in that apartment in Vico Nievo holding the hand of our beloved Cinzia I started to recount, for the first time in many a year, the events that were to change my life forever. It is strange how some things, that are totally unplanned, can determine one's destiny. I cast my mind back to one late evening in the middle December. Christmas was almost upon us and we prepared ourselves for the festive season. My thought were interrupted when through the night air I heard a familiar voice calling "Davide! Davide, where are you?" It was none other than Alfredo Creppi shouting up at Davide's bedroom window! I hadn't seen him in Vico Nievo for months and I ran down into the street and shouted "Hey!" and we were soon greeting each other in the traditional Italian style with a kiss on the cheek and a firm hug. I hardly recognised him with his shadowy beard and he looked nothing like the young fighter I once knew.

"Why are you looking for Davide?" I asked.

His reply was given breathlessly and he was seemed genuinely concerned; "I saw Davide earlier and he was almost in a trance and I thought he was taking a drug or something. He had been drinking too. He told me that he was going to sort out Saverio once and for all. Then he pushed me aside and ran off and I lost him in the Caruggi but he was really messed up!"

I had, of course, some idea of where I could find him and I told Alfredo to leave this to me and I walked off toward the bars and that old stone wall where we had looked at the shooting stars. In the gloom of late evening I found Davide sitting on that old red brick wall looking out to sea. He hadn't even realised that I had approached him and he was deep in thought. Suddenly, he turned startled by my shuffling feet as they crushed the piles of broken brick beneath them. "All right, so what's the problem old friend?" I asked placing my hand on his shoulder. He just shrugged and sat there for a few moments then he said, quietly, "you'll never really understand, even though you are my very best friend, you will never understand!". And he emphasised the word "never" as he spoke. He had never before called me his "best friend" and frankly I felt humbled by it. Then he turned to face the dimmed lights of the bars on the sea front. They were predominantly red, like distant flares, and from within was a muffled laughter that gave away the drunken entertainment from within. These bars were dominated by seamen visiting Genoa and at their service were the local prostitutes. Davide, I knew straightaway, focused on just one of those bars, the Gatto Morto.

Davide opened up his heart to me that night as never before. He told me that he could never get Cinzia out of his head. He had tried to forget she ever existed but he just could not. "Every time I see her face I want to speak to her, be with her, take her away from this!" I had to agree with him that the life of Cinzia had confused even me. She wasn't like other prostitutes, she was a rare beauty with a heart of gold.

For several minutes we sat there and stared, and talked, and stared some more. Davide was clear about one thing. He loved Cinzia and had done for years. He didn't condemn her for the lifestyle she had chosen and held none other than Saverio responsible for everything that had had happened to her. She was, according to Davide's rationale, trapped by him and could never break free! His mission in life was to set her free! Once again we stared at the stars, as we had done when he first told me that he loved her, and hoped that we would see the day when our beloved Cinzia was free from her captor.

As the evening drew late and the bars slowly emptied, the drunks pouring onto the street with their singing and gibberish laughter and we decided to take the slow walk home to Vico Nievo. As we walked we talked some more but, after a short distance, I found myself talking to myself. I turned to see Davide several meters behind me staring once more at that God forsaken bar. "What now!" I called out, but he didn't hear me, totally focused on a big American sedan that had pulled up outside of the Gatto Morto. Stepping out was none other than Saverio and I could feel the blood pounding through Davide's veins as he gritted his teeth in anger. Our nemesis wore a white suit that gleamed against the red glow of the bars behind him. "Look at him" he said. "If only I could..." I cut his sentence short pulling on his arm. "Let's get out of here, we'll talk again tomorrow", but it was like pulling on an anchor, he just stood there refusing to budge. "I need to see her" he said. "That's the reason I came here tonight Tino. That's why I am here". As I looked back at the bar I noticed Saverio was staring across in our direction. Of course, in the darkness he would never have recognised either of us, but he continued to stare all the same. He stooped a little and moved his head from side to side as though he was trying to make out who it was standing there in the gloomy shadows. Then, to my surprise, he started to walk toward us. "Come on" I urged Davide to move, but stubbornly he waited and said "No! let him come". I pressed my face close to his ear and forcefully through gritted teeth I whispered "Davide, this will do you no good, now come on" but still he wouldn't listen and Saverio continued to make his way toward us. Then Saverio's face pierced the shadows and his sneering grin told us that he knew exactly who we were. Maybe Davide had been seen here before I thought to myself. "You've done this before?" I demanded. My words gave away my astonishment but in truth it all made sense now.

Why would Saverio walk over so calmly if he hadn't encountered Davide there before? This time though, it would be different. Davide bent down and picked up a broken old brick. Then he took two quick steps and screamed a roar of anger like I had never heard before in my life, hitting Saverio on the side of his head with all the force of a man possessed. He fell and, even in the darkness, I saw the red blood pouring down his face. I couldn't speak as I was in shock, yet Davide didn't end it there. Crouching over the hapless Saverio he raised the brick high above his head once more and slammed it down violently into Saverio's face again, and again, and again, and again until I grabbed his arm and dragged him off Saverio's motionless, blood covered, body! The suit was no longer white, all I could make out through half light was the bright red of blood and Saverio's staring eyes looking up to the Heavens.

Suddenly I caught a glimpse of a crowd moving toward us from the bars. They were shadows of people that must have heard Davide's scream. Once again I pulled at Davide's shirt sleeve. "For God's sake man, let's get away from here!" my voice giving away the signs of my desperation and fear. At last Davide listened. Together we ran and ran toward Vico Nievo. I turned and noticed that some of that crowd, now at the scene of Davide's attack, had started to follow and their footsteps filled the night air with a frightening echo. "Wait!" I shouted "we can't go back to Vico Nievo, they will follow us there! Let's go this way!" Pointing toward the city centre! We ran for all we were worth toward the Cathedral of San Lorenzo. Surely we could lose them in these meandering streets? Our escape route through those passage ways of the Caruggi that lead to San Lorenzo was occasionally blocked by black market street sellers, prostitutes and transvestites plying their trade. In our panic we just barged our way through them all, knocking over stalls, and picked up a few insults as we did so. Occasionally I looked back until I saw no-one.

After a few minutes, running as fast as we could past the black and white striped Cathedral, we found our way to Genoa's central square, the Piazza Ferrari. We ran straight toward the large fountain that dominates the square and we collapsed onto the small wall that surrounds it. I cupped my hands with water and threw it over my face. "Have we lost them?" I asked gasping for breath.

"Think so, not sure"

"What in God's name were you thinking Davi? These people are seriously bad. You, me, were dead ... " I hesitated as I noticed Davide wasn't listening but his eyes were scouring the entrances to the square. "We can't stay here, too visible" He pulled me up and we started to run again. We ran and ran, past all of the shops in Via Venti Settembre until we found ourselves at the old majestic railway station of Brignole. "Tonight, said Davide, we stay here. Lots of people sleep here waiting for trains, it won't be a problem"

I had recognised very quickly that Davide had said "we" rather than "I". Now, his recklessness had

Senso Unico

involved me. I became angry and grabbed him by both shoulders, shaking him and forcing him to look me in the face. "Look at me! Thanks, friend!" I said. "Now it's we is it?" I shouted as onlookers cast a condemning stare in our direction.

Genoa's station is a huge edifice of stone facing a square with trees and shrubs and there were lots of people rushing about as is normal for a railway station. But Genoa's principal station was to be our refuge at least for one night. We crossed from the park, meandering through the yellow buses and taxis, entering the huge brightly lit entrance hall that was now full of travellers whose voices echoed with the excitement of holidaymakers..

We found ourselves an empty bench, of dark hard wooden lattes, and had been bolted against the wall. In front of us stood a large wooden model, the size of a motor car at least, of Columbus' famous ship the Santa Maria, which partially hid us from the gaze of commuters buying their tickets. We laid ourselves down on the benches and, in some discomfort, watched the bustle of the railway station all around us. I watched as the people hurried by to catch their trains paying little attention to anyone else. There was a group of Swiss backpackers sitting on the floor surrounded by a mountain of rucksacks. There was a lot of noise but my mind was too full of the events of that evening to even try to understand anything. Sooner or later we would have to go back to Vico Nievo, to speak to my mother, to speak to Cinzia maybe, just to do something. For the first time in my life I felt totally helpless. There is a prison in Genoa that is situated not too far from the football stadium and I thought of those high brick walls and how it might be my next home! It was as though my life had just ended right there in that station foyer. Just then I noticed two Carabinieri policemen slowly walking past the ship. They marched together in slow motion with hands behind their backs, their eyes observing all around them, ceiling, floor and corridor. My heart missed a beat and I shoved Davide's leg. Together we stared at them and prepared ourselves to run. But they didn't pay any attention to us and carried on their march towards an edicola to look at the magazines that adorned the little wooden kiosk.

Morning came to Brignole very slowly and neither of us had slept a wink that night!

"We need to go to home and find out what has happened Davide" I said in a soft tired voice rubbing my eyes as I spoke.

"No, they will be waiting for us and watching. Either the police or a gang of thugs, either way it's too dangerous"

"Then, I will go alone. I need to sort something out" I said more forcefully.

Davide looked at me for a few seconds and then replied "you go then. I will wait here for you. Bring some food if you can" Then he looked across at Columbus' ship again and stared at it in deep thought rubbing his chin as he did so. I had no idea at that point what was on his mind as I walked out of the station but it would soon become clear.

Chapter Seventeen:
My Last Day in Vico Nievo

I walked out of the station into the sunlight that for a while blinded me. I crossed the busy street, that was now full of yellow buses, and turned into Via XX Settembre. The street was a main shopping area in Genoa that ran from the Piazza Vittoria and Brignole Station to the Piazza Ferrari and the Port via the Caruggi. The street was full of people. The bars were busy with early risers on their way to work taking that last drink of coffee to get them through the day. The Edicolas[21] were setting up and the street beggars were already sitting on their pavements, a daily Genoan ritual, with hands outstretched for loose change. One old beggar woman, her faced tanned to appear like leather, stared at me as I approached her. I certainly didn't look like I had any money and could only think that they were all looking for me. I was so full of guilt! With every turn of my head I noticed accusing eyes

---

[21] Newspaper kiosks

staring at me. All I needed now was for Caesar to give me a thumbs down and I surely would have died right there. My brisk walk gave me time to question everything that had happened. I wondered why Cinzia had ever turned to the likes of Saverio. It is true that there were pimps all over the Caruggi. The seaport was awash with prostitutes of every age and size. She would have been high class and commanded a good figure and thereby, I rationalised, lies the reason. She, like so many Italians in post war Italy, simply needed the money! Over and over again I sought to justify her actions and I came to the conclusion that she was surely trapped in a world that she wanted to escape from. The killing of Saverio might be her salvation and yet condemn me and Davide to a prison cell. It could be that neither the police nor Saverio's thugs knew for sure who we were. But could we take that chance and stay in Vico Nievo? I soon realised that we were on the run from both the police and the mob!

Soon I crossed the Piazza Ferrari dominated by its huge monastic fountain. There was little traffic and, still meeting those accusing eyes, I crossed towards the Caruggi, passing San Lorenzo Cathedral with those distinctive black and white stripes. Even the lions that sat on the Cathedral's steps seemed to stare at me as I hurried along. Finally, I was in the Caruggi. The smell that day was horrendous. A mix of urine and fish permeated the morning air. Then I saw the gas lamp above the corner of Vico Nievo. I stopped and looked around to make sure that there were no policemen or any of Saverio's friends. The street was in fact quite that day. So I ran to the door fumbling with the keys and practically falling in behind those big green doors. Once inside I fell back onto them for a moment to catch my breath before climbing the stairs to the apartment. I could smell coffee and I could hear the murmuring of a woman. My poor mother, who had been through so much with my father, was now about to be given more heartache.

I unlocked the door and slowly pushed it open. Standing there was Tobia and my mother. She turned in half delight. "Tino" she shouted "where have you been?". I put my arms around her and calmed her as best I could. Clearly, she was not aware of what had happened and no police had shown themselves in Vico Nievo.

"Sit down please, I have something to tell you" I spoke with a low guilt ridden voice. Tobia remained standing throughout my explanation with one arm around her shoulder. Her eyes were wide open with disbelief as I tried to explain. Then Tobia broke my story telling saying "surely, the problem is with Davide. You did nothing!"

My mother answered for me I suppose. "Don't you see? They will come looking for Davide and Tino together! We have to get them away, at least until this has completely blown over". Her prophetic words were about to set a plan into motion!

She stood and grabbed me by the shoulders and shook me as she spoke. "You will go to stay with you

Zia Rosa and Zio Raffaele[22] in Suni!" Suni was a village on the west coast of Sardinia not too far from the small town of Bosa. My mother's plan was simple. She would go and buy tickets for the Tirrenia line ferry from Genoa to Porto Torres in the north of the island. We could then hitch a lift to Suni and stay there out of harm's way. Hopefully, our stay would be a short one, but if we became wanted then we could hide out there for as long as possible. However, whatever the next move would be, Sardinia was the first step we had to take. It had been many years since I lost saw my aunt Rosa and Raffaele. I remembered them as being very religious and wondered for a while how they would feel harbouring a murderer! And they might not take so kindly to Davide? But we had to do something and fast!

It was arranged that we would leave that very evening carrying a letter from my mother. She told me that had no intention of telling Rosa and Raffaele what had actually happened. We were simply on the run from vicious thugs which, in all honesty, was true! It was arranged that we would meet my mother in front of the old Stazione Maritima and leave on the eleven o clock ferry. There was time to pack and I had to return to Brignole and let Davide know what was happening. I packed as much as I could carry and Tobia would bring my two bags, almost too heavy to carry, to the terminal. As I hurried from Vico Nievo it never

---

[22] Zia (Aunt) Zio (Uncle)

crossed my mind that until this day I would never return.

It was also decided that me and Davide would leave Brignole and cross Genoa and stay at Genova Principe. Principe was a railway station nearer to the port and we would draw less attention to ourselves than by spending two nights on the same bench at Brignole. The station is very majestic looking with a huge statue of Christopher Columbus near the main entrance. It seemed darker than Brignole but we soon found a second class waiting room where we could spend the night. I spent most of that night alone because Davide had gone to say his goodbyes and pack everything he would need for the following day. I didn't sleep all night, staring up at the ceiling and wondering what the future held in store. I wondered what Diego would make of it all with his common sense ways, and I grinned to myself for a moment, waiting for the sunset.

Cinzia, enthralled by the detail of my story that she seemed so unaware of, had hung on to my every word and still remained silent about her feelings. She squeezed my hand and walked into the kitchen. "Time for another coffee I think" she said. I was too timid to question her but with a tray of coffee and biscuits in her hand she begged me "tell me more, I must know everything!" and so, I started to speak all over again!

Chapter Eighteen:
The Escape to Sardinia.

With the arrival of the morning came the noise of the traveller. The waiting room was filled with the echo of children's' voices that had little respect for those that were trying to sleep. The station, after all, was no hotel! We had a lot of time to kill, with the ferry leaving so late in the evening, and therefore a long a boring day lie ahead of us. There was time to buy a newspaper, that mentioned nothing of what had happened the day before, and observe the everyday squalor of the beggars that boarded trains to ask for money for a train ticket they would never buy! The day dragged on so slowly that we just sat there, half awake, staring at the bustle of life all around us. In Italian stations there always seems to be someone in a total panic and Principe was no exception! A small bald headed middle aged man in a long grey overcoat was arguing with his overweight wife while their two children just sat there in awe at the spectacle. A missed train perhaps? Or had the wife made a mistake the train timetable? Or was it even his wife? I could only shake my head and afford a smile at Davide who had sat there in total silence, as though in a trance, for most of the night. An old lady pulling a shopping trolley was mumbling away to herself as she hurried by with a face like thunder! These little scenarios, acted out before our eyes, were to form some sort of entertainment as I imagined the stories they might tell. Those that couldn't find a bench to sit on sat on the floor with their cases all around them, as the big wooden clock on the wall slowly ticked away to break the heavy sound of waiting room silence.

Suddenly the huge oak waiting room doors flung open and in walked two Carabinieri with a slow and deliberate stride. These two, and they always seemed to be in twos, were more observant than the officers we had seen at Brignole. They walked all around the room and looked everyone up and down as though they were looking for someone! To leave now would make us appear guilty, and so, we stayed exactly where we were. If questioned we would simply say that we were waiting for a train to Milan where we had relatives. Soon the two policemen were standing right there in front of us. I looked up and smiled at them both as they gazed down at us and then I carried on reading my newspaper as calmly as I possibly could. I felt intimidated, but I stared straight at the page and could only sense their proximity. Eventually they turned and walked away towards the edicola[23] outside. I started to wonder, if we did manage to escape, we would surely be constantly looking over our shoulders for the rest of our lives, and I remained suspicious of every police officer from that moment onward!

As late evening approached we finally made our move to follow my mother's plan as though it were a military operation. We left the station and walked down the long winding hill that leads from Principe to the port. It was just a short distance on foot and soon we crossing the main road to the ferry terminal next to the Stazione Maritima[24]. This big old majestic building dominated Genoa's sea front and is approached by a wide bridge that that crosses an underpass. Behind the building were three ships, all white in colour and the words Tirrenia written in large blue letters that filled their entire length! We crossed the road, weaving in and out of the cars that had started to queue to board the ferries, until we reached the foot passengers entrance; a smaller door to the left of the boat with a long staircase leading to the upper decks. There were people everywhere and a wall of noise greeted us. Somewhere in this mayhem was my mother and Tobia with our tickets, but all I could see was a sea of expressionless faces. "We have to get on board soon" said Davide looking rather anxious "but where the Devil are they?" At that point someone grabbed my arm, it was Tobia. My mother was with him clutching

---

[23] Newspaper Kiosk
[24] Maritime station

our one way tickets. "Senso Unico?"[25] I asked and the reply was a firm "yes". With the tickets she gave me a handful of money which I gratefully accepted. There was just enough time to embrace her one last time. Her head nestled into my shoulder and she whispered "make a better life for yourself Tino. When this comes to pass, make a better life. Get away from the Carrugi and don't ever come back my son". The words seemed harsh at the time but in later years I started to understand exactly what she meant. She clearly saw the Carrugi as a bad place and, like any mother, she wanted the best for her son. What had happened the night before with Saverio had convinced her that the only decent future for us was far away from Genoa. But the pressing problem for now was to get away to safety, a safety that, hopefully, Sardinia could offer us!

Our ship was called the Verga and at the bottom of the gangway was a sign that simply read "Porto Torres". With one last look back at my mother she gave me a smile that in truth was full of sadness. I saw a tear in her eye which she wiped away with her hand and Tobia nodded. At least, despite the differences we had, I knew that my mother would be well cared for. Davide patted me on the back and together we climbed the stairway, looking back after every few steps, until we arrived on the ship's upper deck. Then we made our way to the open deck where from above we could observe the long rows of cars that were moving like a giant dying snake into the bowels of the ship. Then

---

[25] Senso Unico: Lit; One Way Only.

Senso Unico

with a loud crash the giant doors to the car deck closed to the cheers of excited passengers and people were already waving. So too were my mother and Tobia. There was a steady breeze that evening that made standing there for too long a difficult thing to do, but I would stay fixed to that spot until Genoa's lights could be seen no more. Soon the vibrations of the ships engines increased and the deck began to shake. The single funnel gave out a steady stream of smoke and a loud whistle that signalled we were about to set sail. At first the movement was slow, at least slow enough for me to ask whether we were moving at all! Gently, the port side began to slip away and everyone began cheering and waving to the large crowd gathered on the quayside. My mother, my dear dear mother, had her head on Tobia's shoulder as I gave one final wave goodbye. Then, his arm around her, they walked off into the crowd and I could see them no more! That was the very last time I ever saw my mother.

Genoa looked so different from the entrance to the harbour. It looked much bigger somehow, sprawling and weaving its way across the hills, finally fading away into the distance. I could see the old forts on their hilltops and the distant headland of Portofino. We passed an old warship, a frigate I think, and even the crew gave us a wave! As we sailed into the darkness the lights of Genoa grew dimmer and dimmer, fading into the past, just like the life I was leaving behind me. I could just make out the red lights emanating from the Gatto Morto in the distance and my thoughts, for a brief moment, turned to Cinzia. For a long time I could see the old lighthouse giving out its powerful beam; a warning to mariners and a lament for me! The breeze had turned colder standing there on that open deck and we decided it was time to find a good place to sleep. We had no cabins booked and that meant that we had to do as many passengers do, sleep on a chair or even the floor! Staying out there on that deck for so long meant that all of the prime places for sleeping had been taken and we had to find a good quiet place on the floor, if such a thing was possible! There was a small restaurant on board and so we decided that food would come before sleep. I treated myself to something I had never tried before, a Russian Salad, and in truth it was the most disgusting thing I had eaten in my life. Served in a small white plastic container I was amazed that it ever passed for food at all. The espresso coffee that came with it was more welcoming! And so, that was how we prepared for the overnight voyage to Sardinia. Never realising that until this very day I would ever set foot in Genoa again.

Chapter Nineteen:
The Passage to Porto Torres

After the turmoil of the past few days the overnight voyage to Porto Torres offered more than a little light relief. It was in fact the first time I had ever gone to sea. The Ligurian waters were, thankfully, like a pond, still and calm, with the light of the moon drawing a line straight toward the horizon. Though we were still very close to Genoa it already seemed as though I had left many months ago. For the first time in my life I felt alone. Since Davide had attacked the loathsome Saverio he had hardly said a word, often staring into empty space and involving himself in only short conversations. The laughter and humour that he was famous for had for now deserted him. I am sure, and I say this now with an older and wiser head, that he was still in shock and it took all of my efforts to get him to speak.

To my amazement I realised that people were staking their claim to the best possible places to spend the night and I thought we had better do the same! It seemed as though every chair was occupied. Now whole families were setting up their makeshift beds on the floor. Suitcases and rucksacks doubled up as pillowcases and the better prepared had actually brought sleeping bags. We had no such luxury and our suitcases were all there was to give our heads some sort of support. There were two reasons why we would not sleep that night, the bright lights that were never turned off in the room and the constant vibration through the floor from the ships engine. All night it churned away relentlessly showing no sympathy for the weary passenger. We found an empty space next to the bar and set our things down for the night. Together we stared up at the ceiling and my thoughts already drifted to home. I turned to Davide in a vain attempt to make conversation "I think Tobia bought the tickets, I didn't ask, too busy thinking of what we had to do". Davide looked at me and said "we'll pay him back one day" and turned once more to stare at that pale cream ceiling.

I was tired and my body ached, yet sleep was out of the question. How could anyone ever sleep with so much light and noise all around them? Every noise vibrated through the room. Children laughed and a baby cried. A crowd of Sicilians, overusing the word "minchia", laughed and showed no regard for anyone trying to sleep. One of that crowd, a bearded man of about forty and dressed in denim, held up a small silver flask and gestured to us "whiskey" and offered us a drink. He had clearly drunk a bit too much already and I was quick to refuse, politely of course! But he was intent on having a discussion and he talked and he talked. His name was Paulo and he was a Sicilian from Palermo. Every sentence he uttered ended with the word "whiskey" as he raised his flask to toast us both! And now, to make things worse, it started to get very cold.

In the meantime Davide had become more and more withdrawn. His head was in turmoil and his face reflected his pain. He did not even join in the conversation and chose to lie there on the floor with his head resting uneasily on his suitcase. Occasionally he forced a smile when our new Sicilian friend spoke directly at him, but in general, he was in a world of his own. Paulo had packed a bag full of chicken legs and was happy to share them with anyone. I was so hungry, especially after throwing away most of the Russian Salad, that I accepted, only refusing the whiskey flask pressed into my face! The whole night passed by like that and I looked forward to putting my feet on Sardinian soil.

The morning came in a very glorious way and I will never forget it. I walked alone onto the deck, leaving Davide still sleeping on the floor. The sky was a deep red as the sun came up and in the distance, hovering above the blue sea, I could see a wall of mist. It was almost like a child's painting that you find in a primary school[26]. The sun painted a red line on the ocean almost like a pointer towards a better life, or at least I hoped so. The decks slowly filled up with passengers all smiling at the wondrous sight. I heard one man say that Sardinia was hidden in the mist and that "it was always like that in the mornings". The ship sailed straight into the mist, like lost vessels in the Saragossa Sea. As we broke through to the other side of the mist I saw land. I would later see that Sardinia was a beautiful island but my first impression was not so good. Porto Torres was full of factories and long cranes filled the skyline. Chimneys and steel structures pointing toward the sky. Huge silver coloured containers sitting on a red dessert looking landscape complimented by the odd red brick wall. I could see row upon row of containers of every colour. Pipes littered the landscape and there was a quarry. In short, it looked ugly. Soon we would need to disembark and make our way to Suni. It was early morning and it was already very hot. The crowds huddled together in what seemed an almost desperate bid to be the first one ashore! Our old Sicilian friend raised his flask one last time as the ship finally came to a halt on the quay side. Finally, we were in Sardinia.

---

[26] Scuola elementare (Italian)

Chapter Twenty: Nuraghi!

Suni was a long way from Porto Torres and we had very little money between us. Our only hope was to start walking to the outskirts of the town and thumb for a lift. "At least we'll be fit" grinned Davide. The remark was significant because for one split second he appeared to come out of his shell. We walked and we walked until finally we left the port behind us and started to make our way into what looked like a wilderness. As far as we could see there were cacti. It was very green, wild with undergrowth and rocky crags and bushes everywhere. With Porto Torres now well behind us Sardinia appeared to be empty! There was no-one in sight let alone a possible lift. "We have no-chance of getting there like this. It will take us a week" I moaned dropping my old suitcase to the floor and resting my hands down upon my knees. The air was alive with the sound of crickets that had erupted in noise with the rising of that oh so torturous sun! The sweat ran down my face as I stared along that endless road and watched the surface disappear in a distorted heat that rose upwards. I could bear no more and prayed for shelter from that blistering sun and some rest that had been denied us on the overnight ferry! In the distance I could see some old rocks and what looked like a windmill. "Over there, let us rest a while and wait there!" my eagerness all too apparent. By the time we reached the rocks we were almost crawling. It must have been at least forty degrees and there was no shade at all. There wasn't even a breeze to relieve the humidity. As we approached the tower it soon became apparent that it was no windmill. It was some sort of a tower with a small, half demolished doorway, the entrance was blocked with fallen rocks from the roof, but no window to be seen! Yet in the distance I noticed another. "what the Hell kind of people live here that build towers without an entrance or a window?" collapsing to the floor as though I were about to die! From this rock I looked around in admiration of the beautiful Sardinian landscape that was such a contrast with the murky streets of Genoa. With a willingness to abandon our journey in that steamy heat I gazed at a solitary cloud crawling over the top of a distant grey mountain. And somewhere beyond those mountains was Bosa, the Mediterranean, Rosa and Raffaele!

"They are called Nuraghi[27] son" broke the calm as an old man walked around from the other side of the tower taking us both by surprise. "There are more than eight thousand of them" he grinned pointing to the next one that we had already spotted. "Well what the hell are they?" my question interrupted a grunt as I tried to pull myself to my feet. "Nuraghi form a part of the charm of Sardinia, along with the unlimited virgin land and the sea". Clearly this old man was knowledgeable. "you won't find anything quite like this in Italy you know" his words revealing a pride in his country. He sat himself on a rock, falling backwards onto it as though he was as weary as we were, and pulled up his corduroy trousers to reveal well worn old boots. His grin was covered slightly by a large grey moustache and his wrinkled face was probably due to that blistering sun, but at least he wore a cap, which was more than we had! His blue striped shirt was opened to the waist to reveal an aged leathery skin beneath. But he looked friendly and appeared to be the only help we might ever get! "Our first ancestors lived in these towers and yet, they remain a mystery. That next one along this road has an open room where you can get inside and there are old tombs up there too!" His enthusiasm for the subject was clearly apparent. "no-one really knows what they were, temples, houses, defensive towers, who knows?" he said before introducing himself as Paulo, an eighty two

---

[27] The **nuraghe** (IPA [nu'rage]) (plural Italian *nuraghi*, Sardinian *nuraghes*) is the main type of ancient megalithic edifice found in Sardinia.

year old Sard[28] who had only ever left Sardinia to serve his country. "I fought in the Carso at Caparetto[29], there was fog everywhere, we couldn't see a thing. Suddenly they were all around us. I ran and ran down from that evil mountain, it was Hell son, all the way to the Piave River I ran, men just threw down their weapons and ran for dear life, it was a nightmare!" We all knew the story of Caparetto, Italy's greatest First World War disaster, but I had never met anyone that was actually there.

"I bet you saw some terrible things?" my words hoping for even more information. "war is not a game son. There is no patriotic music playing in your ears. People don't die without shedding blood. Hollywood has a lot to answer for!" these were the words of a man that had witnessed many bad things and there was no point in pursuing the story further, he had said more than enough.

He enquired about where we were going and why and he wanted to know where we were from. Our answers were well rehearsed and told half-truths only. "We are going to Suni, near Bosa, to see our Uncle and Aunt and who knows, maybe even find some sort of employment?". To this he gave a short laugh. "Sardinians leave in droves to find work. Most of them go to the mainland. Yet, you two?" he laughed once more! One thing there didn't appear to be too much of

---

[28] A native of Sardinia
[29] The Carso was a region of northern Italy and the scene of fierce fighting in the First World War.

was work and we both knew there would be a limit on how long we could remain in Suni! "Come on then" he said walking to the other side of the tower. There he had parked his old Ape. It seemed natural that this three wheeler pickup should be christened "Ape" (bee). It doesn't look anything like a bee but it sure does sound like one and can be heard buzzing along many a country road. Whatever the name, essentially the Ape was half a Vespa motor scooter pulling a wheelbarrow! Paulo's Ape was a rust colour though shades of the original blue paint showed through. In truth it looked like an abandoned vehicle and we found it difficult to believe that he actually took it onto a road! But then again, this was Sardinia!

"We could pay you to take us to Bosa?" but my words seemed to fall on deaf ears as the old man stared across to the hills. Then, rubbing his chin, he turned to me saying; "I could take you some of the way, but you would have to pay the petrol - in advance!" According to Paulo, Sardinia was full of bandits like the old west! They rode around on horseback and robbed people, vanishing into the yonder hills. "Some", he said with a cheeky grin, "hid themselves in the ruins of old Nuraghe". It was believable. Sardinia was an empty country, devoid of people and an uncultivated wilderness. And so we gave Paulo what little money we had left and stood there for a moment looking at that bedraggled pickup and shaking our heads at what we were about to do!

Alongside the driver there was room for one. That meant someone had to travel on the open flat back with our suitcases! Across the back of the Ape was, mercifully, an iron bar welded into place to store wood. At least this rusting old metal rod would give us something to hold on to, and that we did for dear life! Davide started the trip alongside Paulo and I would do the first stint in the back. As Paulo started the engine there was a stuttering noise from the exhaust and a back fire that frightened the birds from the trees! A cloud of black smoke rose from the rear of the vehicle to pollute the clean Sardinian air! We rolled slowly down toward the roadside, over the rocks and scrub, and then we were on our way. The engine seemed strained at first as though it never got out of first gear, but at least this was better than walking. Within a few minutes we passed the second Nuraghi. I tried to imagine what kind of people might have lived in those towers thousands of years ago. I wondered how they could have possibly etched out a living from this landscape. The warm Sardinian wind rushed through my hair as I bounced around hanging on to the bar as best I could. It was agreed that we would drive to Alghero on the West coast and then follow the coast down to the town of Bosa and then to nearby Suni. The sun was fierce and the wind was warm. Though I didn't realise at the time I was burning, but I was fascinated by that wonderful landscape. Mountains, trees, rocks, long grass, all left to nature and untilled by human hand. Every now and then we saw a Nuraghi. I learned later that the name of these Sardinian Nuraghi derives from the word "nurra" which means "heap" or "mound", but also "cavity". It is perhaps for this double meaning that the word has been applied to the original shape of the Nuraghi, built by laying big stones one on top of the other to create a "hollow" which is then covered by a stone dome to form some sort of room. It was alongside one of these stone wonders that Paulo finally stopped for a break. Each nuraghi was like a milestone, a marker, carrying us nearer and nearer to our final destination.

Chapter Twenty-One:
The Famous Dead Horse!

As I sat in that kitchen with what was now a cold cup of espresso staring into the eyes of our beloved Cinzia, I realised that my telling of the story was, as most people would do I suppose, to be a re-telling of a series of short adventures that dominated the lives that we once had. Cinzia hung on every word with a smile, assuring me that she too would be able to tell me some wondrous things! Firstly, it was time to refill our cup with espresso, and I stood for a while to stretch my aged legs. "You have aged well" said Cinzia "you are still as handsome as ever". That made me smile, I never thought she had ever seen me as handsome! "You are the one who has stayed young Cinzia. Still the girl I always knew!" She settled back into her chair and put her hand over mine and said "Come on, tell me what you did next". I decided to tell her of a strange event that happened on our journey to Suni. It involved something we later referred to as "the famous dead horse". It was something that remained a mystery but every detail has stayed with me until this very day! And so, I began to tell Cinzia the story of the Famous Dead Horse!

On our long rough journey to the small town of Suni we had made several stops. More often than not it was alongside one of the numerous Nuraghi, which, in some cases, offered a little shade from that blistering sun. One of these stops held a mystery that we have never really understood. Paulo had stopped his three-wheeler alongside a ruined Nuraghi that appeared to be in a more state of ruin than the others. On the opposite side of the road I spotted a dusty old path. "Where does that go then Paulo?" believing the old man to know every pathway in Sardinia. "Well son, more often than not they lead to other Nuraghi! Go find out!" and so with his consent I smiled and eagerly set off to have a look around. I soon realised that every one of us must have been filled with curiosity as we all trudged up the hill together following a dusty old path surrounded by bush and rocks.

"Look" shouted Paulo "did you see that?". He had scared the living daylights out of me! "What is it?". Paulo explained that he had seen a polecat run across the path behind him. All I could see was an army of ants meandering between the rocks in long well organised lines. It would appear that there are several animals we might see, explained Paulo, like wild boar or snakes! Now I really felt like we were in the wild and I hate snakes!

On each side of the road there was nothing but thick bush and very soon we were at the top of the hill. From here you could see the world! The warm wind was stronger up there and we could see the sea. so blue and so distant, the valley with wild horses running freely. Without any doubt I felt that we were in Paradise! In the meantime Paulo was picking fruit from the wild bushes. "That will go down well with a glass of Mirto" his broad grin admiring the green fig on the end of his pen knife. Though I didn't realise it at the time Mirto would become my favourite drink too!, and yet almost impossible to find outside of Italy at that time. Mirto is an island specialty that Sardinians swear can only be found on the island. Made from myrtle berries, found predominately in the north of the island, the taste of this liquor resembles a strange mixture of black liquorice, blackberry, and grenadine. The dark reddish liquid is thick and strong and though it is served in a small shot glass is to be sipped slowly, though it may be easier to just shoot it down if the flavour doesn't quite agree with you! It would appear that for Paulo too it was far better than Italian wine!

Further along the meandering path Davide has spotted the ruin of yet another Nurughi. However, it wasn't anywhere near as complete as the Nuraghi's that we had seen en-route to Suni. This one was no more than three layers of stone high and in a much broader circle. As we drew closer it was evident that the sight had been inhabited recently! next to the large circle of stones was a small hut, for want of a better description, made entirely out of the surrounding

Senso Unico

rocks. It was a bit like a den rather than someone's home! There was no window, just a doorway with a rough cloth of dark brown material hanging in front of it and occasionally blowing in the breeze. To the side of the building was an old Volkswagen Beetle. The boot was half open and grass and weeds were growing all over it. Under the bonnet was a wasps nest with so much activity that we all stepped back sharply. David called out "hello" and repeated his call several times. All I could think of was the stories of bandits living in the hills and this place had a strange feel about it! All the while the hot sun beat down on us and the air was filled with the noise of crickets. In the distance I spotted another herd of wild horses that roam Sardinia. They raced through the distant meadow and their beauty brought a smile to my face.

Next to the hut was a large enclosure. This too was built roughly out of the old rocks that scattered the ground. On one side of the enclosure was a small hill that would give us all a good view of the surrounding countryside. From the top of the hill I glanced once more at those distant wild horses. Then to our surprise, as I turned back to check the enclosure, I spotted the corpse of a decaying horse. It must have once been an elegant animal as its hide still shone a healthy chestnut. Now there were just empty sockets where its eyes had once been. Its hind legs were crossed and ants crawled all over it. Strangely, the horse was still tethered to a post wedged into the rock. The questions were soon to follow. How could this happen? How did this happen? Did the horse starve to death? Who and where was the owner? None of us had any answers but we were sure that the answer was within the hut. Once again Davide called out "Hello! Hello!" But there was no reply. For all of our courage no-one had the nerve to enter that stone hut. All we could do was to walk away, occasionally looking back, as though we were leaving the scene of a crime! "What if" said Davide, followed by a long pause "there is someone dead inside?". It seems plausible that the owner of the horse might have died and hence the horse starved to death! The possible causes were discussed with passion as we walked swiftly down the hill and back to the pick-up. We drove away staring back up the hill wondering what story that old nuraghi might have to tell. As for Davide, he was as aware as myself that we had to keep a low profile here in Sardinia, so going to the police was out of the question. To this day I have no idea what had happened on that hill and I thought, from time to time, about whether that old horse was still lying there, and whether the owner was inside his hut, sitting there decaying like the horse in the enclosure. I thought about those wild horses running free and how they contrasted with sad animal we had just seen, tethered to that post with so much grass beyond that stone wall! In the months that followed we would often discuss the horse and perhaps, after my belated return to Genoa, I one day might go in search of the truth. After that, whenever the horse came up in conversation, one of us would say "not the famous dead horse story again?" and so it became known as exactly that; the Famous Dead Horse!

Chapter Twenty-Two: Suni.

After a long and gruelling journey from Porto Torres, Suni appeared on the horizon like an oasis in the desert. Lots of little white adobe houses with red tiled roofs sitting amid a green countryside of rolling hills and beyond that the beautiful Mediterranean Sea. A 15th century Church, which I later discovered to be San Pancrazio, rose up high above the terracotta roofs. We had finally arrived and I hoped and prayed that we were not bringing them trouble. Here we would have to disappear and hopefully one day soon return to Genoa; la Superba[30]!. I had already started to miss my city more than I could ever have thought possible. Now we had to say goodbye yet again, to the kind old man Paulo that had driven us so far in his trusty old three wheeler! We exchanged addresses and vowed to let him know from time to time how we were getting on. Maybe we could even pay him a visit one day.

---

[30] Genoa is known as La Superba: Lit the Superb!

Senso Unico

Paulo dropped us at the top our street, Via San Pancrazio, that led to church we had seen from a distance. We had now just a short walk to Rosa and Raffaelle's house. In truth we never heard from Paulo again and often spoke of his kindness that day. The last time I ever saw him was driving off with a cheery smile and wave.

We walked a short distance and soon we were at my uncle and aunt's villa. It looked a typical 17th Century farmhouse with a small garden filled with flower pots standing on barren ground amid the constant thrill of the grasshopper. Outside was a large marble sink fed by a green hose pipe. I didn't realise at that moment but this was where we would have to wash every day! As we walked along that street the Sard women were sat on small chairs outside of their front doors. They were predominantly dressed in black and smiled as passed. I would imagine that strangers did not happen along too often in Suni! Then Rosa and Raffaelle appeared together at their door. Rosa was dressed like the other women; head to toe in a black dress that emphasised her grey tied back hair. She was much smaller than I remember her but she had the loveliest of smiles. With a tear in her eye she called out my name "Tino! Tino!" and rushed over to give me the biggest hug I have ever had! Raffaelle was much calmer and looked every bit the gentleman! He wore black trousers, which had seen better days, held up by braces over a blue striped shirt. His moustache was huge and completely hid his mouth! But here stood a proud old gentleman, a man who had served his country, and now he etched out a living in this backwater Sardinian village! He spoke like a General in a very clear and precise manner that left little to any doubt about what he intended to say! We were, as one might expect, visibly tired and our appearance prompted Rosa to immediately get us both settled in. I presented Davide to which they cordially gave him a kiss on both cheeks in the traditional manner. He was made as welcome as I was and we entered their home as if it was our own!

The house was very odd in its design. The front door, which was really a side door, led on to a long half-lit passageway. Most of the rooms were on the left with two large doors, double width, on the right. The first led to the kitchen where most of the time they seemed to live. The Kitchen was dominated by a long heavy wooden table adorned with a huge vase full of freshly cut flowers. Rosa always loved to have plenty of flowers in the house. The rough whitewashed walls were shelved and an old doorless pantry covered by a long beige coloured cloth separated it from the main room. At the end of the corridor was our bedroom. There was just one shuttered window which muffled the noise of sheep that appeared to us to be in the far distance. I opened the shutters to see that the street was now full of sheep. The shepherd seemed to be drowned by them all and he glanced at me. He was old with a leathery face and his smile revealed a set of very unhealthy dentures. I returned his smile with a nod and half closed the shutter once more. So this was it, a little bit of paradise that in truth was to be my prison. I laid back on the bed and stared at the ceiling with

Rosa's monotonous voice, a failing of hers that she could never stop talking or giving advice, ringing in my ears. "You'll be all right here the two of you". She was right, there was enough space for us both. The two single beds were ample and the single wardrobe was more than enough for both of us as long as our stay was a short one! Soon the letters started to arrive from Genoa. One letter included a newspaper cutting, that we did not show to Rosa and Raffaelle, from the Genoan daily paper il Secolo. It read "Gangland Murder" and described Saverio's killing with a brick. At least we now knew that Saverio did not survive. There had, according to my mother's letters, been strangers lurking in Vico Nievo. Two men had apparently been seen watching our house. They had spoken to no-one and generally just stood there on the corner watching everyone as they passed by. Once they were seen talking to Cinzia and that was proof enough that these two were in league with Saverio and the Gatto Morto. Clearly an early return was out of the question and we would have to exploit Rosa's hospitality to the full.

Chapter Twenty-Three:
As Time Goes By

Soon the days in Sardinia turned into months and the months soon turned to years. The 1950s was a great time to be alive and I spent many leisurely hours listening to American singers like Frank Sinatra. For almost two years we lived life to the full and grew into young men on that magical island. Our only contact with Genoa was through a steady stream of letters that arrived on a weekly basis. Mother had finally married Tobia and I was told to stay away from their big day, which, apparently, was for my own good and I was not even told about it until the wedding had actually taken place! That had been my mother's idea as she was sure that a wedding, known to all in Vico Nievo, would attract the wrong kind of attention! They had married in the local church with just a handful of guests to witness it. Diego and Alfredo had turned up uninvited in the hope of seeing me once again! One letter included a photograph and my heart sank thinking that I should have been there. There were even strangers in the photographs and that only made me feel worse!

In the meantime Davide had found employment in Bosa working at a local Cinema as a projectionist. Bosa was only a short distance from Suni and the pay gave him a good living. Around the house he turned into an excellent cook and I thought his real vocation in life was to be a chef! However, he seemed contented with the lifestyle but always appeared a little distant. In truth I had learned to live with the situation we were faced with far better than he did. His conscience was his ball and chain and I suppose that knowing you had taken a life is hard to bear. As for myself, well I could fare no better than working at a small bar in Suni. The bar, named after its owner Gino, was very small and frequented predominantly by the old men of the village. But the work was steady and helped me to contribute to the household of Rosa and Raffaelle.

The bar owner was a character the likes of which I have never met since. He was in his mid 50s and totally bald, of small stature with the biggest smile on the island. Throughout his life he had lived with, married, divorced, lived with again and now friendly with what seemed to be hundreds of different women! He was constantly entertaining some female or other leaving me to man the bar alone. Age was no barrier to this predator of women! I suppose, in some strange sort of a way, this gave me some kind of job security! Gino loved to brag too and all of his exploits were eagerly reported to whoever would listen in the bar. It was difficult to understand just what sort of woman he was looking for as they came in all sizes. Some were small and thin whilst others were large roly-poly types. I once asked him what he looked for in a woman and he simply replied "a pulse!" I suppose that summed up Gino. He always referred to his women as if he owned them. One he referred to as "my Barbara" and he spoke of her as though she was the most beautiful woman on the planet! You can imagine my shock when I saw her for the first time. She walked with a heavy limp and had a hump back! I could only try to keep a straight face not wanting to offend anyone, but I wondered why he had never mentioned it before!

Gino was passionate about football, as most Italians seem to be, and we had lengthy arguments about the National Team. He was a supporter of Cagliari and would sometimes make the train journey to see home games. I was supporter of Genoa, and therefore a Genoano, but Davide was a Doriano and therefore supported Genoa's other team Sampdoria. This often led to a lot of leg pulling and rivalry between us, particularly on those late evenings sitting in the square.

My time in Sardinia was one of growing up and reflection on what might have been. My life was boring if I am truthful and I stumbled through the same old routine day in and day out. I enjoyed going to the small square in the evenings where a young Sard, a 17 year old who looked more like a gypsy, would play his guitar as we sat around looking toward the Heavens for that odd shooting star. Now that was entertainment and my life carried on in that way until one evening I noticed the most beautiful vision I had ever seen cross the square without giving me a second glance. Who was she? I had to know. I asked everyone and no-one replied as I was met with a wall of shrugging shoulders. She was petite with auburn hair brushed back and plaited with a single heavy plait at the back. She had the face of an angel with big bright eyes and the loveliest of smiles and she wore a blue and white dress, looking as though she was going to a ball! Yet she crossed my path and headed toward a waiting car which sped off into the night. I wondered then if I would ever see her again but surely I would. I am shy to be honest, and certainly not so bold at speaking to strange girls, but in my mind I orchestrated and schemed how I would speak with her, that is, if I could only find out who she was!

I went back to square every night after the bar had closed and often sat there alone but she never returned and I eventually I gave up all hope of ever seeing her again. Then, late one Sunday evening, under a clear star studded summer sky, I sat in the square listening to the music, laughing a joking with Davide and a handful of friends we had met over the years and she appeared once again. She had walked from a small house that she had been visiting and briskly walked toward the same waiting car. I simply had to find out about this girl and I jumped to my feet and followed her muttering under my breath words that might get her attention and not make me look stupid!

"Excuse me – errm excuse me!" I called out timidly. She slowed and turned looking bemused at my intervention. "I am Tino, are you from here?" Thankfully, she smiled, "no, I live in Cagliari but we have a summer house in Bosa and my grandfather…" she stopped short. "Why do you ask?" After a moment of nervous hesitation all I could say was "Oh, well, I don't know really" what a silly answer I gave, it wasn't in my plan at all! And she smiled and turned away again. "But wait!" I called out "I didn't get your name!" "Carla, I am Carla, Carla Tubertini" she replied with the loveliest laugh I ever heard, and with that she was gone with a small wave and a broad smile. At last my vision had a name!

While I was telling this story I noted a broad smile on Cinzia's face. "Why the smile?" I enquired and to that she just shook her head and said "I can't see a ring on your finger Tino, did you ever marry?" I just shook my head and gave a smile that confirmed my bachelor status. "After Carla there was no-one else" I said. "What about you?" I enquired noting that she was wearing a ring. "That is a story for later Tino and besides I need to hear about these things that are all new to me first!" I wondered then whether I had overstepped the mark a little and her husband was long dead. And so, with a raised eyebrow, I continued my story.

The next time I saw Carla was in church. Every Sunday Raffaelle woke me early to go to Mass. More often than not he would inspect how smart was my

Senso Unico

appearance before we set off and mutter something under his breath that indicated it would do – but only just! I always wore a white shirt which was the best piece of clothing I possessed! The shoes had to be shone so as to see my face in them and the same applied to Davide too! And so it was on Sundays that the four of us, Rosa, Davide, Raffaelle and myself, walked the short distance to San Pancrazio, arriving early and sitting in the same pew, three back from the front. I always sat next to the aisle with Raffaelle next to me, and then there was Rosa and Davide on the other side. This would stop us talking during the usually long sermon that father Bartholomew would always deliver. His voice would echo around the church and at times was incomprehensible! As the service was about to begin with the organ sounding a few undistinguished notes, I noticed several people sitting in the row on the opposite side of the aisle. Soon I became transfixed; it was her, the girl of my dreams, Carla. She wore a white silk scarf, as it was the custom in those days for women to cover their heads in church, which blew slightly off her shoulders due to the breeze from the opened doors. This time she wore a beautiful white dress and looked every part an angel. Next to her was an elderly gentleman of seventy or so in a black suit, his hat sitting on the pew behind him, as we all stood awaiting the arrival of the Priest. I stared at her for some time until she finally acknowledged me with a smile. Father Giuseppe broke the silence "in nomine patre et figlio santi" I crossed myself and stared at her again. She was the most beautiful girl I had ever seen in my life and she didn't even seem to have any interest in me. At this point Raffaelle had noticed that I was paying little attention to the service and he gave me a hefty shove in the ribs. The whole service continued like that and I wanted to see her at the end, but Raffaelle had his ritual to attend to and that meant I did too; we lit a candle and prayed for distant relatives and those that had passed on. By the time I walked out of the church she had gone and I was left alone once more. I briskly walked and ran to the square and sat myself on a bench opposite her grandfather's house. I waited and waited until it became dark but she never showed. Then I saw a light go on in the upstairs window. It was Carla moving across the room and I stood up hoping to get her attention. Then she reached out to close the shutters only to hesitate for a moment looking at me and appearing surprised to see me there so late. I waved, she smiled, I smiled and then she closed the shutter slowly, never taking her eyes off me! I am not really sure what kind of impression I had made but at least she saw me and she did smile!

I decided that I would sit out in the square until she came and spoke to me. Then I might ask her to go out with me, and who knows, she might even say yes! I have always found rejection difficult but I knew I just had to try or I would lose her forever. I sat there for a long time and the silence of the night was deafening. Eventually, feeling tired and dejected, I walked home kicking stones with my hands in my pockets like a scolded schoolboy. Cinzia pulled at my sleeve as if to get me out of a trance as I recalled that troubled evening. "Life is like that Tino" she said "Some things are meant to be and I am sure that there is a reason for everything in God's great plan." She smiled "Life is senso unico" [31] There was a pause as she said that, and then she urged me to tell her what happened, and why I remember so vividly a relationship that didn't, at this point, seem to be going anywhere!

That old square in Suni was not just reserved for the young people to hang around in. It was frequented by all ages and many of the village's old folk would meet there to reminisce, to share war stories and reflect on the brevity of life. One of those that came so often was Raffaelle. He would sit on an old wall and talk with his friends. Perhaps they too did this when they were young men. The square always had a buzz and there was always laughter and conversation there. Although I got along really well with Raffaelle I never confided in him my innermost thoughts. Yet, for some reason, that evening I did exactly that. Maybe the loss of a father figure and my unhealthy, for that is what it now seemed; infatuation with Carla had forced me to turn to him in desperation. I knew I had to get her out of my mind as she was simply not interested and I had done far more to attract her attention than I could ever have imagined. The evening was beautiful and the stars filled the clear Sardinian sky. The tranquillity of it all was broken by inquisitive words "so what is on your mind young man?" It was Raffaelle. He had wondered

---

[31] Lit: a one way street.

over, leaving his own friends, because he had become concerned at seeing me sat alone staring at the Heavens with a worried expression written all over my face!

"You wouldn't understand Raffaelle" I said turning away as I spoke.

I tried to shrug it all off at first but he wasn't to be ignored so easily. "Take a chance, tell me! I know there is something on your mind and it's not that Saverio business either! Is it something to do with Davide?" I was never quite sure of how much Raffaelle knew of what happened in Genoa. His reference to Saverio brought back a painful memory that momentarily took my mind off Carla.

Then I reassured him that the problem was not anything to do with our past, to which he sat himself beside me saying "well it's a woman then! You are the right age and all of us go through this at some point!"

"Raffaelle" I stared straight at him "how do you know so much?"

"Age, wisdom, I served my time and I too had my dreams. Those dreams cannot be fulfilled sitting here in Sardinia getting old like me!" To that I thought it better to tell him about recent events and how I could not understand my own feelings. He told me that "part of growing was not always getting what we wanted. Sometimes, even though we might not want it, we have to settle for something else, something less even". I started to listen with deep interest to fragments of his life story and how he had fallen in love himself with a girl from Verona when he was serving in the army. I heard of how he would sneak out of barracks to meet her and everything was going well, until her father caught them together in an old barn! "Nothing actually happened" he reassured me, though he might have been economical with the truth on that point, but her father had chased him with his stick and would surely have killed him had he caught him! "Did you see her again?" I eagerly enquired. "No, I was too afraid to go back" he said. "Oh, I would have, I could never leave it like that!" but my answer to that was just raised eyebrows and a shake of the head. He stood up and put his hand on my shoulder and slowly walked back to his friends saying quietly as he walked "don't stay out too late Tino, get some sleep tonight".

Raffaelle was right. I stood up and kicked the nearest rock as hard as I could, so hard that it flew right to the other side of the square. I rested my arm on a tree and my bowed head on my arm. It was like my world had just ended and then I heard her voice. At first I thought it was just a figment of my imagination and then I heard it again; "Tino" she said gently but I couldn't let her speak. "You are the most beautiful girl I have ever seen. I know how strange this all might seem to you but I think I love you" to that she just gave a short laugh and a big smile "more beautiful when you smile too!" I was now committed and there was no turning back. "Tino, I would love to see you, I know how you have waited so long in the square, but the truth is it could never work. I study at the

University of Pavia, I am studying to be a doctor one day, and my parents stay in Cagliari but they are planning to return to Rome where my father works. We come here in the summer months to visit my grandfather now" Carla's grandfather was the elderly conservative looking gentleman I had seen in the church. "When would I ever get to see you dear Tino?" she put her hand on my cheek as she spoke and I found myself looking straight into her eyes. Soon, without prompting, we drew closer together and I kissed her. This was very much out of character and I don't know where I found the courage but I actually kissed her. It was nothing heavy or passionate, just a tender short kiss on the lips. As she drew back, her eyes moving up and down, she said "I hardly know you Tino. I don't love you, I am older than you I think and I know these things. We can write if you like and one day …" before she could finish I said "Yes, and I will wait". We sat together on that old wall, her head on my shoulder and my arm around her waist. It was the most romantic thing that ever happened to me and I have never got over it. She said that she did not love me but she acted as though, one day, she might!" That tiny spark of hope was enough to make me feel happy!

In the days that followed we met several times. We would take the bus into Bosa and walk along the marina hand in hand. We would swim and lie on the whitened beaches drinking granita[32]. She would often wear a brown coloured bikini that radiated her

---

[32] A flavoured ice drink

loveliness all the more. I was in love for the first and only time in my life. This summer was wonderful and I wanted it to last forever.

Chapter Twenty-Four: A Change is Due

My summer was a perfect one without doubt and I thought it would go on forever. I started to forget that I was in affect in hiding from Genoa's gangland thugs and that my circumstances were entirely due to the actions of Davide. Back in Genoa my mother had informed everyone that we were travelling the world and that she had lost touch with us. Our situation could not, at least in reality, continue like this. Meeting Carla only made me crave for normality! The lira[33] that we earned was always a cash payment or black money. We never paid any tax and we were not even registered to vote. Davide and I knew that sooner or later we would be required to complete our national service[34]. The youth of Italy

---

[33] Italy's currency at that time.
[34] La Leva (Italian)

Senso Unico

were required to spend one year in the armed forces at that time and failure to turn up could mean imprisonment. If we didn't show there, are some that might say it was an admission of guilt. If we did show, mobsters in Genoa could easily track our whereabouts and we might end up face down in a ditch somewhere! I knew all of these things were about to happen but for now all I could think about was Carla. Soon she would leave for Pavia to carry on with her studies and unless I returned to the mainland I might never see her again. My head started to spin thinking about the situation we were in once again!

One evening in our room I finally managed to discuss things with Davide. He seemed content with living the good life forever on the island and didn't have any feeling for going back. For a long time now the strange figures that haunted Vico Nievo, the two gangsters often seen hanging around and mentioned in so many letters, had not been seen and the law had never called to interview us. I confessed to Davide that "Now might be a good time to go home again?" To which he just shook his head and frowned looking at me in disbelief!

"Tino, I know what I did has wrecked your life and I am sure that at least you might be able to go back but the risks are greater! I can never go back as there is nothing for me but misery and danger. To see that girl, he chose on this occasion not to use her name, ruin her life at the hands of pimps and put myself in danger. No, I am better of living this secret life here. I would just end up killing someone else!"

I assured him that "as time goes by they will forget what happened in Genoa" and then our thoughts turned to the national service we would be required to attend. The letters would go to our home addresses and we would, without any doubt, have to report in Genoa!

Without hesitation I told him "I am going back". I had planned that I would return when the letter arrived but not before. Davide, on the other hand, would avoid the order and continue to live in hiding in Sardinia. All I had to say was that Davide was still travelling and I did not know where he was should anyone ever ask me! We had a plan, a little rough I admit, but it was a plan! I still had a girlfriend that "liked" me rather than "loved" me but time, I was sure, would open her eyes. We still had to discuss our plan with Raffaelle and secure a home for Davide. Once he had been requested to serve his country they might not be so eager to give him accommodation, especially once I had left! My concerns then turned to Carla and the sort of future we might have together. In all of these years that have passed since those troubled times I have looked for Carla in every woman I have met, but she is never there! Cinzia appeared to be on the brink of interrupting my story at this point and then, after a brief pause, begged me to continue, which I did.

Two days before Carla was due to leave for Pavia the dreaded letter finally arrived. As expected I had to attend a medical, as was normal at that time, and deciding on what branch of the forces I would serve in, Italians could request their preference without guarantee in those days, and I decided I wanted to serve in the Alpini and go to Pavia at every opportunity. Now I all I had to do was to tell Carla, a task I was dreading, and say goodbye.

The rain poured out of a cement coloured sky the day Carla left for Italy. It was fitting really that the day was so miserable and we decided to meet in the square at midday, shortly before Carla's grandfather was about to take her back to Cagliari and to her parents who had left a few weeks earlier because of work commitments. I waited for her under a large tree that offered me good protection from the rain that never seemed to ease up. I leaned on the tree looking up to the sky where a sudden flash of lightning made me think twice about standing where I was! I moved slightly away as the ground shook with thunder. Carla changed the mood as she ran into me with her coat pulled over her head and laughing as she threw her arms around my neck and kissed me as though we might never kiss again! There was a small bar in the square and we made a dash across the open ground to get inside. Two espressos and a seat by the window, where we could stare at each other, hold hands, and make promises that would never be kept. Raffaelle walked past the door and exchanged a brief glance at Carla, smiled, and gave her a nod as though they had some sort of secret between them. "What was that all about?" I asked to which she replied "nothing". But there was a guilt written on her face that day!

When it was time for her to leave we stood in the doorway and we held each other tightly. I thought she would never let go. Then, she pushed me away with both arms, frowned as though she was about to cry, and ran off towards the waiting car that had already sounded its horn to hasten the proceedings! I remained in that bar as she left, staring at the car as she drove away. As it drove off down the street Carla stared out of the back window blowing a kiss, smiling, and miming the words "Goodbye" and "I love you". That was the first and last time she ever said that she loved me as I never saw her again. I watched the car disappear in the distance. She was gone. I didn't realise it then but Carla had left my life forever. I walked home a lonely figure in the pouring rain, kicking the stones along the dusty road, with my hands in my pockets like a scolded schoolboy. I felt empty as though my world had just ended. I half expected Carla to come running back round the corner or maybe she would be there waiting at the house for me! As I entered the house Raffaelle threw a towel over my head and muttering something that frankly I cannot remember. Now I too had to prepare for my departure from this, my prison, and yet my paradise.

That evening I didn't go to work. Instead, feeling sorry for myself, I just lay on my bed staring up the ceiling, examining every crack and cobweb. Within the next week I would have to pack my case and make the long awaited journey back to Genova. At least I had that to look forward to even though it was fraught with danger. I didn't sleep much and Davide came in without saying much. I suppose he understood how I felt. "Are you all right?" he enquired and I replied with a nod and a smile but my body language clearly stated that all was not well. "Goodnight then" he said rolling over to face the wall and leave me alone once more with my thoughts.

Chapter Twenty-Five: A Farewell to Suni

The following morning the rain had stopped and, as I opened the shutters, the street smelled fresh and clean. There was a cool breeze and a peaceful serenity prevailed. Davide suggested we go to the beach in Bosa and relax a little. It seemed the best option and might stop me moping around all day as I was already missing Carla terribly. So we took the short bus ride down to Bosa Marina and lay there on our towels and smothered ourselves in sun tan lotion. Here too the breeze brought us some relief from that unforgiving Sardinian sun. The beach was crowded, as it often is in the summer months, and we were grateful for the small space that we had found! Occasionally we made a dash over the hot sand, which burned our bare feet, to swim and the blue tranquil Mediterranean waters. It seemed that nothing could spoil such a beautiful day!

The, one of the local boys that used to hang around in the square, known as Sam but I doubt that was his real name, came sprinting breathless across the crowded beach, weaving his way through the maze of towels that seemed to completely cover every grain of sand. He was a skinny young boy and his slight frame was emphasised by wearing just baggy white shorts and sandals. "Found you" he called out but he was so breathless that he could hardly speak. He didn't really need to say a word as it was clear that something really bad had happened. Collapsing on the sand he recounted events back in Suni while we had been lazing around on the beach. Two men had been walking around Suni showing photos of myself and Davide all day. They had been asking questions of everyone in the village. I recalled that my mother's letters always spoke of two men in the street and I wondered whether these two were the men! The news was not slow in finding its way to Raffaelle and at the very moment that Raffaelle had dispatched Sam to find us the two strangers appeared at the house. One of them was a giant of a man, well over six feet tall, and wore a white suit that made him stand out. The other was a rough looking man in a black pin-striped suit but he had a shoddy unshaven appearance. As he walked away from the villa Sam had witnessed them kicking the door and one had grabbed at Raffaelle's throat. "There was a lot of shouting" said Sam; his words trembled as he spoke. "Raffaelle said you were not to go home. Go to the Nuraghi near the beach and wait there!" The orders seemed clear enough and so too was the cause. It was bad enough losing Carla and getting my country's call ... but this? Saverio had finally found us, even in death!

It was now abundantly clear that a return to Genoa was out of the question. I became concerned for Raffaelle and Rosa! Sam only heard the shouting and did not witness anything that followed. I was afraid, both for myself, Davide and my Uncle and Aunt. Davide was convinced that we should return and confront them but, through fear I suppose, I thought it best we shelter in the Nuraghi and ask Sam to return to Suni for more information. All we could do now was to wait!

We lay there that night with our heads resting on damp rolled up towels. It was really cold and the Nuraghe was lit by a bright moonlight. I thumped a clenched fist at the ground thinking that once again our lives had been shattered by events in Genoa. I had little heart to run away again and even if we did where could we go? Davide remembered that he had brought some food in his rucksack, just a little cheese and a couple of bread buns, but it was a meal to remember. We spent a sleepless night waiting for Sam amongst the rocks of the crumbled Nuraghe and finally, in the early hours of morning, He arrived peddling for his life on an old borrowed bicycle. He looked as though he hadn't slept either and opened up a brown paper bag of focaccia[35]. He also had a big bottle of orange juice. I didn't realise at the time but the food we ate at

---

[35] Flat baked Italian bread topped with herbs and other ingredients.

the Nuraghe was to be one of the last meals that we ever ate in Suni and I would never return to thank Rosa and Raffaelle for all that they had done for us both! Then Sam handed us a letter, clearly written by a shaky hand, explaining what we had to do. Raffaelle had told the intruders that we had left days ago for Porto Torres looking for some work. Sam said that he had never backed down and didn't tell them anything and in return he received a black eye. The thought of them attacking an old man sent a shiver down my spine and I gritted my teeth with anger. I wanted to go back and kill them both there and then! There had been several witnesses to these thugs entering Raffaelle's home and, with the story circulating now in the small hamlet of Suni, the men had already left town. Some people thought they had gone to Porto Torres. Raffaelle had, at the very least, bought us some time! Over the next few days Raffaelle had sent us a steady supply of food, sleeping bags and clean clothes. It was agreed that we should not return to Suni as our two visitors were violent and intent on revenge. Now all we could do was to wait. Communications came in regular brief notes on scrap paper and we hung on to every word. Raffaelle was forming some sort of a plan and as soon as it was completed we could make our move!

The following morning we were surrounded by a thick mist, the sort that blanketed the island in the summer months, which shrouded us in a protective veil. In Sardinia, and I suppose in many parts of Italy, the one person who could arrange anything, the one person with total confidence of success, had to be the Parish Priest. And so it was to be that early, wet, misty morning on the outskirts of Suni. Lying there in my damp sleeping bag I noticed the outline of a man walking toward us in a haze of fog. He drudged his way along the road and seemed to be visible long before the bicycle he was pushing. We both partially sat up, not knowing what to expect, when he called out my name! "Tino" We both now sat up and through the cloud appeared a friendly face. "Tino! Davide!" It was Father Bartholomew[36], the old parish priest from Suni. He was very unlike our local priest back in Genoa; very quiet, always calm, a serene smile. He wore small square glasses that sat on the end of his nose and he seemed to only ever peer over them. His grey hair, he must have been around sixty year's old, swept back with brylcreem from his forehead. His eyes betrayed a kindness and an understanding of all worldly things. Both myself, and Davide, had little idea of just how much this man knew and we both hoped that Raffaelle had been somewhat economical with the truth about our situation.

In Sardinia it is more often a case of "it is who you know rather than what you know". This is how things are done there! It is said that a parish priest can arrange everything you need and even help you find work! Few could say no to a priest! "Ah boys" he called out to us "how wonderful to see you both! My journey in this weather was not so pleasant", he shook his head as

---

[36] Bartolommeo

he spoke and sighed, "but you are both safe and that is all that matters" It is strange, but I have always felt safe in the presence of a priest. Davide was much less religious than I was so I doubt he felt the same comfort. The old priest put his hands on my shoulders as we both scrambled to our feet. "You are going away boys!" he smiled as we looked at each other bemused at what he had said. Raffaelle had only told him part of our story and he thought, in all of his innocence, that bad people wanted to harm us both, and on that point he was right! He then passed us a piece of paper that was crumpled and torn from the pocket of his long black coat. Written on the paper was an address with the name Marco Bertini in bold letters. I asked who he was and I was told that he was the Priest's brother now living in New York. "In truth, he is not a religious person and you wouldn't think we were brothers but he is a good man with Christian morals" and he explained that he had long forgiven his older brother for running off to the America without really saying goodbye. Now they were once more in contact by letter and telephone and, even though he had never met us before, he was willing to help us on the other side of the world. It was agreed that a return to Suni was too risky and therefore a car, a taxi that was paid for by the priest, would collect us and take us to Oristano. From there we would take the train to Cagliari where Father Bartholomew had arranged for us to work our passage on a ship, the Dorian Sun, bound for New York. There we would be safe, adopting new names if necessary, and disappear forever. I have to admit how much I regretted accepting that decision. Now, I had not only lost my country, but also my very own name. I was told that there were lots of Italians in New York and nobody would ever question us. We could apply for citizenship as relatives of Marco Bertini and we would be safe. I was hesitant and wondered for a moment how a priest could do so much in such a short space of time. Such is the power of the Church. So, reluctantly, we agreed to go to America, where my life would fester until this moment, the day I returned to Vico Nievo.

Chapter Twenty-Six: Cagliari

The following morning an old yellow taxi pulled up alongside the Nuraghe that had become our temporary home! The driver was so short he could barely look over the steering wheel. Through the opened window he called out in a squeaky voice. "Oristano", almost like a bus pulling up at a scheduled stop, and he made little attempt to get out of the cab. "Yes, Oristano" I replied with a hesitant smile. "Very well then, throw your things in the back with those two suitcases. Raffaelle said your things are all there inside". Upon my word, our Uncle had worked hard in securing our freedom, packing our suitcases in advance, and so, within just a few minutes, we looked back at the Nuraghe, now fading away into the mist of early morning, and another adventure was about to begin. "Your documents, and a letter for Ship's captain, are all inside those cases" squeaked our driver and with that we were on our way. My heart sank as I stared at Suni in the distance and I thought of that first time I saw those little red roofs sitting among the green Sardinian hills. Once again it was time to say goodbye and I wondered if I would ever get to see dear Raffaelle, whom I had grown to love as a father, or indeed Rosa and Suni again! Part of me wanted to stay and fight and part of me was very afraid. One moment of madness from Davide had once again forced us to flee a place that I had come to love, and now I freely admit that I was feeling bitter and angry with my old friend all over again! I looked with sadness out of the rear window until I could see those roofs no more. The morning heat had started to distort my vision of the road surface and so I closed my eyes and tried to get some much needed sleep.

Oristano, a place I had never been to before, appeared in the distance. We passed fields of sunflowers stretching skywards to face the sun. I noticed old medieval walls and a Moorish looking tower sitting over the town. It didn't have the grand scale of Genoa, or the quaintness of Suni, but I was relieved to see it. We travelled through the town with its quiet meandering streets until our station appeared through the trees on the far side of the piazza[37].

At this point of my story Cinzia squeezed my hand tighter than she had done before. "You poor things, all of this trouble because of me. I was never worth all of this. Don't think I have never suffered for what you have been through, for what you both did for me"

---

[37] Town Square

Senso Unico

Cinzia's eyes welled up with tears as her guilt began to show. In some way I knew then that what had happened that night on Genoa's sea front affected us all for many years. But Cinzia didn't want to talk about herself beyond her feelings. "My story will be told too, be patient" she said begging me to continue. And so I did.

We had to wait hours on that platform, sitting there on a concrete bench staring across the empty tracks. A strange looking character stood close to us and stared at us through icy eyes. He was young and thin and wore a long overcoat unsuited to the heat. "Have you got a cigarette" he asked with a strange drooling voice. I informed him that neither of us smoked but he frowned and repeated "please" several times. I doubted his sanity and just reiterated that we didn't smoke. Once again he said "please" much to the annoyance of davide! "Fuck off!" was Davide's reply and this had a much better response than my efforts had produced. With that the strange young man walked away and stood at the far end of the platform. We were then joined by a Neapolitan family. There were grandparents, mother & father, three children, all loud and complaining about one thing and another. Here, acted out before us once again, was the panic found in all Italian railway stations! They were soon followed by the lovers! It was hard to tell who was staying and who was leaving, but they seemed to devour each other in passionate kisses. She was very pretty and reminded me a little of Carla. Slowly our quiet platform had become a hive of activity as we waited for out train ride to freedom. The post war economic crisis, unemployment on the island, and the forced militarization of the island territory (70% of Italian military bases were located in Sardinia) aggravated the crime rate. Sardinians, let alone ourselves, were on the move. Many moved to work in the Industrial triangle of Northern Italy[38] and others moved further afield. It seemed to me that everyone was trying to escape from Sardinia in those troubled times.

Finally our train arrived and was by now greeted by a platform full of eager passengers. There were only two carriages pulled by a large green diesel engine that ground noisily to a halt in front of us. We soon filled up the seats of the tiny carriage and settled, if somewhat uncomfortably, into our seats. The platform was now completely emptied as the train sat there taking a rest from the unforgiving Sardinian sun. Leaning on my hand I stared out of the window. Davide was sitting opposite me and he too looked wary and tired. Then, at the very moment the train had started to pull away, I noticed two men rush onto the platform as though they had missed the train. One wore a white suit and the other was an unshaven giant of a man. Their piercing eyes scanned the train and then I realised who they were "It's them! It's ……" Davide creaked his neck turning to see them both as the train pulled away at walking pace. "Another minute and they would have had us both!" my words left my

---

[38] The so-called Industrial Triangle comprised Genoa, Milan and Turin.

trembling mouth with some relief and expected anxiety. Davide gave an icy stare at the larger man and held his hand up, as though to wave, then made a fist and raised his middle finger with a broad grin! With that the two men ran out of the station and were undoubtedly heading for Cagliari! "Well now what?" I enquired. "The rate this thing travels they will probably get there before us!" Davide was calmer than me. "We just carry on as though nothing had happened. Sardinia is not easy to drive across, we'll get there first!" Soon I was staring at the Nuraghi that passed us by for the last time. I saw a fox scavenging among the rocks that surrounded one of them and those magnificent wild horses racing through a field. My Sardinian paradise would soon be in my past.

The train was hot and had no air conditioning. All of the windows were open and the air that entered was warm and gave little relief. Occasionally I would wipe the beads of sweat from my brow, struggling to breathe in that cramped carriage, our journey to Cagliari was anything but pleasant.

Cagliari surprised me. I had never been there before, despite our time on the island, and I expected a sprawling high rise city like Genoa. After all it was the Sardinian capitol. It was nothing like Genoa. There were no high rise buildings and it appeared to me to be a larger version of Bosa. I had a good chance to make my observations as the train made its way slowly through the city. Soon we slowly pulled into the station and how relieved we were to finally set foot on terra firma once again.

Raffaelle had put a letter in the case to be handed to the captain of the Dorian Sun. He had also drawn us a map of how to find our ship. The ship was exporting Sardinian cheese, a speciality called pecorino[39] cheese made from ewe's milk and known for its salty taste. Pecorino Romano is probably the best known outside of Italy, especially in the United States. It was also exporting specialized machine parts from Genoa, the ship's port of origin. Personally I disliked pecorino immensely. So once again we gathered our belongings and struggled to make our way through the crowds on that long platform. We carried a suitcase each, sleeping bags and small rucksacks, so our pace was laboured as we buckled under the weight of excess baggage! Yet despite this burden we decided to walk to the port. On our map it all looked so very close but in truth we moved at a snail's pace and it seemed like miles. We passed the city's main piazza creeping its way up a hill that ran from the sea front and slowly, but surely, we made our way along Via Roma, Cagliari's main street that bustled with tiny shops and small café. Looking up I noticed the most beautiful auburn haired girl looking down on to the street from a small window. For a moment she reminded me of Cinzia with her large brown eyes and constant smile. I wasn't really sure if she was smiling at us or whether she was just a happy sort of person. She was obviously aware of my

---

[39] Pecora – Sheep.

attentions as I couldn't take my eyes off her. Then I thought of how impossible our situation was to ever consider any kind of serious relationship. We were on the run from mafia type thugs and always would be. And so by crossing a wide main road we arrived at port. By comparison with Genoa this wasn't the large dirty port we had come to expect. This port was clean and bright and looked more suited to tourism than trade. By now we were almost dragging our cases under that relentless Sardinian sun. My shirt was wet with sweat and I felt as though I could walk no further. But the sight of the port encouraged us to complete our undertaking, even though we stopped every few yards to take a break! After a few enquiries we found ourselves staring at the Dorian Sun.

Chapter Twenty-Seven:
A Brush with Genoa

Dorian Sun[40] was a strange name really, an English name with a Genoa reference. I later discovered that the ship had been built in Scotland and later registered with a Genoan shipping company. So I suppose the name made some sense in the end. She was an old survivor of the last war and looked as though she had seen better days. The bridge lay square in the centre of the ship rising above two flat areas for storage either side. The single funnel was to rear of the ship and either side of the bridge were two large masts. The ship's hull was rusting and didn't look seaworthy but this was to be our home for several weeks or so. One can only imagine our excitement when we later discovered the ship's journey was to call at Genoa to be loaded with precision machinery before we sailed for New York. This part of our journey would be fraught with frustration as we would not be allowed ashore.

---

[40] Andrea Doria was a famous 16th Century Genoan Admiral.

Senso Unico

Any ship coming from Sardinia would be under the keen observation of Saverio's hoods. And so we were introduced to our ship in the port of Cagliari and, like all of our homes before it, we were to remain hidden just yards away from our parents and friends as I would finally get a glimpse of home. As we stared at the Dorian Sun we wondered about the crew and her captain. Slowly, and apprehensively, we dragged our luggage up the long wooden gangway to the greeting that was to await us at the top.

Before us stood a giant of a man, standing with his legs apart and hands on his hips and the sternest eyes I have ever seen. He didn't say a word, but his piercing eyes sat on top of a full white beard and he glared at us as though we were not welcome. For a moment there was pause as we all appeared to wait for the other to speak, and so, I mumbled and swallowed and fidgeted enquiring "are you the captain of the Dorian Sun?". He didn't answer but walked around us inspecting everything about us. "Have you ever done a days work in your life?" he growled sarcastically. "Yes sir" I replied timidly revealing nervousness from within. "I" he emphasized "don't believe a word of it" and he cranked his neck toward us and stared straight into my eyes. My thoughts turned to leaving the ship and heading somewhere, anywhere, as far away from this man as I could. Then I remembered the letter and fumbled through my pockets to find it. "Erm this sir is for you. It is from my uncle in Suni, near Bosa, and …" He stopped me from saying anymore by putting his finger over my mouth as though I were a scolded schoolboy! "I know who you are boy. I know both of you!" Then he turned his back on us and called over one of the crew, a small thick set man with arms covered completely with tattoos. "Show them where they sleep, or should I say hide, because when we get to Genoa you stay there and don't come out!" There was silence as we followed our tattooed colleague. We had just had our first encounter with Captain Giuseppe Bruno. Throughout our journey he mellowed visibly toward us and was as frightening as he appeared on that first day!

Like most of the crew our tattooed crew member was clearly from Naples and spoke with that familiar Neapolitan accent. "My name is Michele but everyone calls me Mikki" he said with a grin. Then, as we were about to go below decks, he stopped and pointed to a fat man sitting on a pile of old rope. He was huge and wore a sweaty looking white vest that didn't even cover his large stomach. He was unshaven and a cigarette hung loosely from his lips. "Now that is Cagan!" he said in whisper. "Never mess with that one! He never mixes with anyone!" It was then that I started to wonder how, in all of my life, I was constantly confronted with anti-social morons. Why is it, I thought to myself, couldn't everyone be friendly and just get us through this life unscathed! And with that we finally made our way below deck.

The cabin was dark and had six bunk beds that were like shelves, surrounding a fixed table, hidden by a little red curtain. This cupboard, for it was no more than that, was to be our home for the next two months. It was hot in the cabin and would be difficult to get any real rest there but we had to accept what was offered to us for free.

The crew of the Dorian Sun was fifteen. A collection of the strangest characters you could ever wish to meet. There were two brothers' Enrico and Marco Spano. Like most of the crew they had originated from the back streets of Naples and spent the best part of their adult working lives at sea. Most of their days were spent falling out with each other and on occasion they even resorted to fighting, having to be separated by whoever was closest. Brawls would start over nothing and yet they were inseparable. The captain found their behaviour something of an entertainment and often he would just grin and shake his head at the first sign of a scuffle. There was of course Mikki and Cagan, and then there was Corry. He claimed to be born in the USA but he couldn't speak a word of English. He was in his early 40s he had a thick head of black shiny hair and combed it every five minutes; a comb was always visible protruding out of his shirt pocket. He had never married but told countless stories of his many encounters with different women in different ports. The sea was the only life he had ever known. Then there was Stinky. I wasn't familiar with his English nickname at first but it soon became the first real English word I learned, apart from Hello and goodbye. Stinky told us that his ambition was to break wind "like a pig sty". A strange ambition that we believe he achieved many times over.

He had this strange ability to break wind at will. It was always loud, without any care about who was close by, and the smell was awful! On many occasions this short, bald little man with a broad grin that seemed to be wider than his face, would break wind in the cabin during the night. He did this with a forced grunt and it was often followed by a churlish snigger! The solution was to get your head under the covers as quickly as possible! He would even resort to walking over to where you were working, breaking wind, and then walking away laughing! Yet despite his vulgarity I liked him and his wicked sense of humour.

It had occurred to me that between myself and Davide we knew about a dozen words of English, most of them words that could not be used in everyday polite conversation! I decided to try to read English at every opportunity, opportunity that presented itself in the captain's collection of classic novels, all written in English. I was fortunate enough to have access to old English to Italian dictionaries, and night after night on our long voyage, I would read a paragraph of English searching for every word in the dictionary. My simple rational was that although I might not speak English with any fluency I could, with a lot of hard study in advance, make myself understood. And so it was that I started to read David Copperfield by Charles Dickens. It took me about a week to work out the foreword alone, but very slowly and with a lot of frustration, I felt as though I was making progress. I learned that despite the stern appearance of our captain he had a heart of gold and was always happy for me to borrow his books.

The following morning the Dorian Sun finally pulled away from dockside and we started our voyage, our escape, once more. Slowly we stared at our beloved Sardinia and watched as it disappeared into the mist, much the same as it had appeared to us when we first saw her, until only distant hills, as though painted on an old canvas, were visible above the cloud. I was saddened to see the last of Sardinia and yet thoughts of seeing Genoa again excited me too. In conversations with Davide I had even considered sneaking ashore when we arrived in Genoa to see my mother but the dangers were far too great. Cinzia looked at me and smiled as I said that. "You did the right thing to stay on that ship Tino" she said. "There were men who had vowed to avenge the death of Saverio. I know because I heard them say so". I was astonished at her open honesty, an honesty that had betrayed her darker past, and a past that now seemed so full of regret. I continued.

The voyage to Genoa lasted just one night. We busied ourselves with menial chores like washing the dishes after lunch, cleaning windows and storing old rope. We watched the sun set before we went to our bunks and I lay there with my hands behind my head staring up at the wooden ceiling above me. The ship's engine had a constant drone that affected my sleep, just as the ferry had done when left Genoa for Porto Torres, and yet I soon began to ignore it and fell asleep exhausted. After breakfast with the crew the coast of Italy was now visible on our starboard side. In the distance I soon recognized the headland that jutted out into the sea. This was unmistakably Portofino. We stared at the coast of Italy like two school boys going off on a summer vacation. "Look that's Rapallo and Santa Margherita!" Davide's enthusiasm matched my own. But soon our spirits were dampened with a few words from our captain who was also staring at the coastline. "You can look but you're not setting foot off this ship!" I was dismayed but understood that we could never go home again, no matter how much we wanted to. "If I could only go ashore for a few hours" I said turning to look at Davide "or maybe we could get word to someone and they could visit us?" Each question was met with a shake of the head and a frown from the captain. "If those hoodlums get wind of you being on board, and they already have suspiscions after our ship left Cagliari, you are dead! And I think you both know it! Now be patient and keep your heads down while we are in Genoa. And that's an order!" And so we leaned over the ship's side and gazed at those special places where we spent our youth and then, as we rounded the headland of Portofino, sprawled from the port to the mountains that surrounded it, was our beloved city. "Look, there's the old lighthouse and the forts on the top of the hills"[41] we laughed. "It looks more beautiful than ever" said Davide. "I think it is because we haven't seen it for so

---

[41] Genoa is surrounded by old Napoleonic forts that guarded the city from attack.

long. They say that you don't know what you have got until it's gone!" My words were true I know for I have missed my home city more than words could ever say. My home-coming in old age was a day I had dreamed of all of my life. These words brought a smile to Cinzia's face and she stood. "I want to hear everything. You're going nowhere Tino so sit there and I will make us a drink with biscuits". Cinzia's return caught me daydreaming a little and I felt lost for a moment, lost and somewhat lonely. The passage of time does that to some people and I had grown more thoughtful as time went by.

As we approached the dock I was filled with mixed emotions. I felt elation at the sight of Genoa, and despair at not being able to set foot on my home soil. Little had changed since we had been away. There was still that sea of shuttered windows staring down on the square of Caricamento. Old medieval arches intermingled with shops that fronted the port. There seemed to be cranes everywhere as though they were going to rebuild everything, to restore a city damaged by the ravages of war. Then there was the beautiful Banco San Giorgio adorned with a huge mural of Saint George killing the fiery dragon.[42] How my spirits were lifted to see that again! As we slowly made our way into the port we sailed past two huge signs that read "Silos di Genova" and from this point I could look toward the Carrugi and Vico Nievo. The Caruggi looked more inviting than ever and the streets bustled

---

[42] San Giorgio was world's first bank.

with people rushing around everywhere. Many of the front streets are covered with old medieval arches that give it a particular appearance that other cities don't seem to have! If only I could get a message to my family and friends I thought to myself. If only I could slip ashore and see everyone again. My thoughts turned to how we all sat around the dockside as children, chatting, singing, throwing stones into the water and looking at the big ships as they sailed out of that magnificent port. I was, even though it was for a short time, glad to be home!

All day we stayed below decks, though the need to go and see my mother was eating me up inside, listening to the loading and bustle of the dockside. Through a small porthole I could stare at those passing by. Now and then I would see someone in a suit, now synonymous with gangsters, and my mind turned to Saverio and his bunch of hoodlums that had caused us so much pain. I wondered too about Cinzia and whether she had now forgotten that we ever existed. A re-assuring squeeze of my arm and a shake of her head reassured me that she had not!

The night-time was no better, I was tempted to go ashore, more determined to take a risk! The dockside was quiet and dark. I could be home and back within the hour and I told Davide that I wanted to try it. Davide put a hand on my shoulder and told me calmly that we had made a promise to the Captain and, if we did go ashore, he might change his mind about taking us to America. "Think Tino" he said "Think of New

York. These people will kill you if they catch you". It was tough but somehow, with the persuasive words of Davide constantly ringing in my ears, I stayed there on the ship. I did at least manage to sit on the deck and watch stars, as long as I kept my head down! I could hear the distant strains music breaking the tranquility of the night, a French singer I think with a voice like Edith Piaf, playing in one of the Carrugi's bars. I could see the light flashing across the sea from the old lighthouse and I could dream that I was home and safe once more.

I remember lying there all night on that deck looking up at the stars. In the half light I watched as clouds formed faces. I imagined them to be the dead staring down at me from Heaven in judgement. They all looked stern and bearded and old. I searched eagerly for one friendly face but there wasn't one to be seen! Occasionally I caught glimpse of a shooting star and I remembered how we used to sit out at night looking for them! Diego was the keenest spotter, so much so that we thought he made them up! How I wondered what he was doing at that moment, probably already tucked up in his bed, just a short distance away from our ship.

At this point Cinzia interrupted my story. She told me that Diego had died very young. He had become a banker of high repute, attended business meetings, drove a big car, earned a lot of money, smoked big cigars, drank wine and was very overweight. She told me of how he had bought a beautiful rooftop apartment close to la Piazza della Vittoria but spent most of his time in Milan. He had suffered a massive heart attack one morning whilst getting ready for work. Diego was just forty years of age and the first to pass away of the Vico Nievo gang. The story brought a tear to my eye and I too could recount my own experience. At the age of 57, whilst living in America, I too had suffered a heart attack. I remembered sitting on the stairs, thinking I had a bad case of indigestion, sweating profusely and phoning for an ambulance. I lived alone and so I had to make the call myself. I remember that the ambulance arrived within just six minutes, which I am sure was a blessing. I spent the following week in hospital. Nature had rebelled and I had to slow down a lot! Friends took care of me in the weeks that followed. I had even played five a side football just the week before and felt in good health, I didn't smoke or drink and I cursed God for the deal he had given me. I suppose that in it was during this turbulent period of my life that I made a conscious decision to return to Genoa at some point and declare my exile over! I spent six months recovering from that and, despite my initial anger at God; I started to attend church again. Being a Christian has given me a lot of comfort in my old age and I never miss Mass on Sundays.

Cinzia had begged me to continue with my story after stating her sadness at hearing about my illness. I showed her the packets of tablets I now had to take and then told her of the sorrow I felt at leaving Genoa for a second time. The lighthouse waved me a final farewell as we left in the early morning. Just as when we left for Sardinia I watched from the deck and I said goodbye to the Caruggi, to San Lorenzo, san Giorgio and Vico Nievo.

Ahead of us lay the great ocean as we sailed past a British warship standing guard in the Straits of Gibraltar. Next stop was America, a new life and a new beginning.

Chapter Twenty-Eight: America and the Intervening Years

The voyage was a long slow and laborious one. I spent most of my time laid there in my bunk reading my English books and trying to pass away many a boring hour. We had work to do of course, cleaning the galley and the decks, tiding up and helping with any maintenance job that we were given. I would stare out at a sea showing no sign of land, just a flat horizon on all sides, an un-nerving sight that I had never seen before. Even sailing from Genoa to Sardinia offered the sight of distant land. The further we sailed the chilled winds worsened and life on deck was horrible. Corry had a unique way to kill the boredom. He would sit on a pile of old rope and carve small wooden animals out of wooden sticks. He called this "whittling wood", a phrase he had picked up in America. His favourite was to carve a seal sitting on a rock. The smooth body of the seal contrasted with the roughness of the rock. When he had completed one he would give it to someone for luck! In fact he even gave one to me which I carry to this day! At this point of my story I pulled the carving from my trouser pocket and showed it to Cinzia. It was as fresh as the day it was carved. I thought about painting it once! But Cinzia assured me that its original state was far better and had a certain attraction that paint would hide.

As the weather worsened we worked on deck with little woollen hats pulled right over our ears and the rain came at us sideways. I hoped that at least New York would be better, and so, every day we scoured the horizon for our first sight of land. And then, one foggy morning, it finally happened. There she stood in the mist, to many she was a beacon of freedom, a symbol of everything that America stood for, Liberty[43]. She appeared in the distance standing on her island and seemed to give us a welcoming wave! Beyond lie the tall buildings of New York. I had never seen anything so magnificent in all my life. The buildings stretched to the sky. I gazed at Liberty once more and thought to myself, maybe, just maybe, we will at last find our freedom. I thought of all the immigrants to this new land that must have thought as I did as they too left oppression behind to find a new life. She was my symbol of hope and I was prepared to do whatever I could to have a good life and try to forget, no matter how difficult, the life I once had in Italy. I now stared into Cinzia's eyes and said "I wanted to, I really did, but I could never settle really. I often thought of Carla,

---

[43] The Statue of Liberty

Sardinia and the Carrugi". In my dreams I was often running through those long narrow streets and getting lost in a myriad of old buildings. I was desperate to see my friends again and I grew all the more lonely for not being with them.

We docked on an old pier with wooden planking, hailed as we entered by a barrage od ships sirens, that had become slippery in the drizzly rain. Soon, we were surrounded by tall buildings, cranes and ships of every size that seemed to park themselves right here in the middle of town, or at least that is how it seemed to me! The pier was a hive of industry with people running around everywhere. Americans, I thought to myself, were very loud people! It had been arranged that we would wait on board our ship for one Marco Bettini to find us. I had just a brief description of him so all we could do was to wait. We prepared our belongings and watched as New York life erupted with a wall of noise beneath us. We waited for hours and started to wonder if Signor Bettini would ever come.

On the packed dockside one old gentleman really stood out in the crowd! He waddled, rather than walked, along the portside on bow legs and he had a very crooked back, yet despite that he was brisk as he made his way along the quay. He wore a tweed jacket and a matching flat cap beneath which was a traditional Sardinian white moustache. Like many old people of his age a lifetime was etched into his bronzed face. This was surely Marco Bettini.

Senso Unico

The old man made his way through the crowded pier as though he was on a mission. He walked rapidly at almost a run, constantly looking up at the ship and the two of us staring right back at him. Then he stared at me and shouted "Tino" and repeated it several times. I looked at Davide and said "how does he know that I am Tino?" I waved and smiled as he made his way hastily up the gangway, tripping as went, and almost falling onto the deck. Marco Bettini, we were soon to discover, was a man that could never shut up! He had the incredible gift of asking a question and answering it before you had time to answer!

"And you are Tino, I've heard all about you from that brother of mine. Of course you are Tino, exactly as he said you would be. Welcome to America!" His words were spoken as though he was in a hurry and only had a limited time to squeeze them all into a sentence. He put his hand square into my back and thrust me to the side of the ship. "Look out there Tino, what do you see?" As I mumbled an answer describing the pier he cut me short "No Tino, what you see out there is opportunity!" I just stared a while "Look again, this is not Italy. Work hard, succeed, and earn money!" At this point I thought it time to introduce Davide and turned saying "this is ..." Once again Marco spoke before we could say anything "Ah yes, I've heard all about you too" sounding a little sarcastic, and somewhat rude, as he spoke. Then Marco thanked the captain, a man we had come to know as a friend despite his harsh appearance, for all he had done for us, and we in turn shook hands with the whole crew that had a lined up behind him like a guard of honour. One by one we embraced each one of them with a traditional Italian kiss on both cheeks and a firm handshake. As we were leaving the ship I heard someone break wind. Stinky grinned in his usual childish way and all I could do was to shake my head and smile. So we left the Dorian Sun with a heavy heart and we carried, and dragged, our overloaded baggage trying to keep up with scurrying Marco Bettini. Almost running, as he knew no other way, we scampered along the along the old wooden pier as quickly as we could.

Marco was a very extravagant character and this reflected in his choice of motor car. American cars looked huge and we tossed our luggage into the "trunk" with ease! He drove a 1951 Cadillac Coupe de Ville in pure white with bumpers like battering rams. I sat in the front and Davide, somewhat subdued after his short conversation with Marco, sat in the rear. Marco could hardly see over the dashboard but soon we found ourselves driving in a queue of traffic permeated with bright yellow taxis. "We are going to Brooklyn" he said with a smile "that's where we live!" After a long drive we arrived at Marco's apartment. The building was magnificent and outshone all others in the street. A tall red brick apartment block with big windows and four towers on each corner that resembled a medieval castle keep. "Don't worry" he said reassuringly "we live on the ground floor"! Marco later informed us that he always wanted to live on the top floor like the desired residences in Genoa or Milan

Senso Unico

and he dreamed of having a beautiful terraced garden. However, apart from this desire he seemed to have everything that anyone could possibly wish for. As we entered his apartment it was like entering a palace. It was spacious with many rooms leading off wide corridors. The furniture was all Italian, smoke glass tables, high back chairs, drapes that covered the windows all the way to the floor, walls filled with photographs of family and fresh picked flowers. Marco's restaurant had to be doing very well to live in this comfort I thought to myself. A room had been prepared for us both in advance and two colossal wardrobes were assigned to each of us. The floors in our room had been covered in brown Italian marble and shone beneath our feet. We were told that the arrangement was temporary and that one day, sooner rather than later, Marco would expect us both to find our own way in the world. That was understandable seeing as were not even related! He then reassured us that he would never abandon us and would help us settle well into a new life. Constantly he would repeat the word "opportunity" and he meant it. Left alone in our room we felt like millionaires. I had never seen such splendour. The beds smelled of roses and a large window helped bathe the room in sunlight. This was living!

On Sundays there was always a family get together. Marco's wife Moira was an amazing cook and worked at the Marco's restaurant. Although she was American she had the appearance of Sardinian woman. Her hair was a dyed jet black and she was very stout! She would adorn herself in black clothes to match, just as they do in Sardinia, and she made every effort to speak Italian whenever she could. In the kitchen she ruled and everyone had to leave when she was cooking, but she turned out masterpieces in cuisine every time. Cooking was both her work and her hobby! They had two children, both with Italian names, Franco and Maria. They too were very large obese children. Maria was about twenty years of age and would wonder around the house all day in a long dressing gown that looked like a tent on her. Franco was basically lazy. He seemed to just lie out on a sofa all evening and read or listen to music. He would wear shorts in the house and I was always fascinated by the sheer size of legs. He was much older than Maria, by about five years or so, and like Maria, he worked at the restaurant which was clearly a whole family affair!

There was also an Irish employee that worked as an accountant for Marco. Her name was Catherine but everyone called her Cat. She had big green eyes, just like a cat, and a beautiful Irish accent. Over the years this beautiful Irish girl became a close friend. She was to become my advisor, my confidant, my ally and soul mate. I was invited to her wedding to one James Coupland, a New York banker and her lifelong love. I remember thinking at the time how I wish all girls had this girl's temperament; the temperament of an angel without a bad thought for anyone. I was very lucky to find a friend like Cat and we remained friends for many years to come!

Senso Unico

In the evenings, or at least in the beginning, Davide and I worked at Marco's Ristorante Italiano. The restaurant was very big with lots of round marble topped tables adorned with candles. The floor too was white marble and the whole place shone of cleanliness; I am sure that if you wanted to, it was possible to eat your meal off it! I either served tables or cleaned the floor or washed the dishes. Davide, who was always an excellent cook, having learned much of his trade from Rosa, excelled in the kitchen. Every evening the restaurant was full and clearly had a very good name. Cat would call in with a pile of black ledgers and disappear for while with Marco in his small office. Life would settle down for us both and for the first time take on a semblance of normality.

Eventually, after just a few months in fact, we managed to have our very own apartments. Marco, who was now regarded more as family than a friend, would even call and chat after work. There were girls too, but I could never find the woman I was really looking for. I had a problem that was never obvious to anyone that I knew. Every time I met a woman I lost interest very quickly after comparing her with Carla. It was, after all, Carla that I was looking for in someone else! How I often wondered where she was and whether she ever thought of me! Although he never said as much, Davide I am sure was constantly thinking of Cinzia too. I reminded him on one occasion that she was a few years older than us and was probably married herself by now. That only made him frown and for a brief moment I thought he would shout at me or worse!

There were, of course, women in my life. For a time I lived with a Spanish girl called Pamela. She was very small, about five feet or so, and had long thick dark hair that reminded me of Cinzia. Her hair was so long that she could actually sit on it! But, despite her prettiness, she had a fiery Latin temper. I grew accustomed to having objects hurled at me, for the most trivial thing, from across the room and she was even prone to slapping me. One day I came home to discover a plastic model vintage care that I had painstakingly built smashed on the kitchen floor. That was enough for me, the last straw, and I left her. Then there was Loretta. She was a New Yorker of German origin. Like Pamela she too had long hair, though reddish in colour. She was much taller and far more athletic. When she wasn't at her Yoga class or jogging, or roller skating, or kick boxing, all that she wanted was sex and more sex. She tired me out but at least she didn't throw pans at me! As with Pamela, our relationship came to an abrupt end! She had started seeing someone else, a fitness instructor that worked in the local gym where she trained. To be honest, I didn't love either of them, but I was still young and life was something that would last forever.

As time passed we eventually went our separate ways. I was seeing less and less of Davide as our own affairs dominated more and more of our time. He lived on the other side of Manhattan in a small bedsit and his visits became less frequent.

I decided to move away from New York and make my fortune in Texas. I had applied for, and was successful in being offered, a lucrative job working for a popular Dallas Newspaper. We said our final goodbyes at the Grand Central Station, a station that reminded me of Milan, full of architectural magnificence. Marco was there too. He gave me a long hug and we promised each other that we would keep in touch, as people do, and to visit whenever it was possible. Davide, half smiling, had a tear in his eye. "I'm sorry Tino" he said "sorry for everything I put you through" and he meant every word. "It was all me, my selfishness, my stupidity, and you paid for it" I stopped him from going any further. I assured him that we were brothers for life and there was nothing to forgive. We just stood there for a moment and looked at each other before he threw his arms around me and I did the same. I felt a wrench in my heart as though a long friendship had ended, as though someone had died and I felt like I would never see him again! Yet something drove me on to leave. I boarded the train and leaned out of the window as it slowly pulled away and I watched as my two dear friends faded from my sight for the very last time. We wrote of course and I heard that Davide too had moved to Baltimore and was busy running his own small restaurant there. I hoped and prayed that he would find the peace he so richly deserved and that we could meet again one in better circumstances.

My journey took me south, firstly by train and then by bus. I managed to see a little of Washington DC on a stop-over before making my way to Plano, a suburb of Dallas, in Texas. I bought a small house with a large back garden and a few trees. Here in Dallas I would etch out a career in newspapers. I sold advertising space to local businesses for a small tabloid newspaper. Through the many contacts I made in advertising I had a wealth of friends and for some time life was full. I was good at my job too and I eventually became manager of a Property Newspaper and found a new hobby; photography! I frequented the bars, the cinema, and the restaurants and became a fan of baseball. I even managed to secure a mortgage on a bigger house in the centre of town, but I never found the ideal woman to fulfil my dreams. Those dreams stayed in Italy and I knew that one day I would return.

Over time I witnessed so many things. In many ways I became an American. I even took part in anti-war marches protesting about the conflict in Vietnam. I was a little old for the draft, an American word for conscription to serve in the armed forces, but I wore a peace symbol on an old ex-army jacket and wore my hair long with sideburns that reached down to my jaw. I was in awe at Neil Armstrong set foot on the moon, the Beatles changed music forever, and I was in the crowd that cheered John F Kennedy in his open top limousine moments before his was shot in Dallas. I read with interest about the actions of terrorism in

Italy, about the Red Brigade[44] and the Assassination of the President, Aldo Moro. I even managed to get a copy of Il Secolo, Genoa's daily newspaper, from time to time from Danielle, a friendly Neapolitan newsagent. But Italy, Sardinia and even New York now slept in my past and I was engulfed in the day to day ritual of everyday survival. I only ever visited those places in my dreams now and Davide had lost contact altogether after he moved to work in San Diego.

One day a letter from Sardinia informing me of my mother's death after a short illness. I cursed that I was not able to attend her funeral, and in fact it had already taken place before the letter arrived. She, like my father before her, had been suffering with cancer and I never even knew it. She had requested that I was never told in the hope that I stayed away. I thought of my father's last moments and prayed that her passing was not as painful. As I folded that letter and put it away in a draw it felt like that was my goodbye.

---

[44] A terrorist organisation based in the north of Italy.

Chapter Twenty-Nine: The Final Chapter – Revelations!

Cinzia sighed and fell back into her chair. She seemed exhausted by my telling of events. "I am so relieved to hear what you, and in particular you, had to say about our past Tino" she said with a shake of head. "But why, after all these years did you come home?" I noted a wry smile across her face as she uttered these words "of course, I am so pleased that you have! What do you think of Genoa now you are back then?" I answered Cinzia's first question by telling her that ill health and growing old made me want to see my home at least one more time. I had actually made the decision years before, lying there in that hospital bed after the heart attack. During my recuperation I had an allergic reaction to aspirin and for a while my health seemed to deteriorate. Then I started to have doubts about travelling on an aeroplane, which I was not allowed to do for some months! I suppose I then slipped into retirement and spent more time in my garden as retired people do. "At least you have a garden!" she said with broad grin and a touch of jealousy. "I didn't expect to find anyone left Cinzia" my words bringing a hint of a tear to her eyes. "Finding you has been ... well ..." she stopped me from finishing what I was about to say by ending my sentence for me "family". She was right. I considered her to be closer to me than anyone I ever knew in America. I told her that it was about a year ago that I started to plan my trip and thoughts of coming home had dominated my thoughts every single day. "You made it" she replied and all I could say to that was "yes I did!"

I flew from Dallas Fort Worth airport via Memphis and, especially for someone as old as I am and that hates to fly; this was an extremely long journey home. My first sight of Genoa, a city I last saw as our ship pulled out of the port sixty years earlier, was this time from the air. I could clearly make out the port and the Tirrenia Line ships, still sailing from the terminal close to the old Stazione Maritima, though the ships looked very different now. As my bus passed them later that morning I noted that they were a lot bigger now, still predominantly blue in colour but now they were adorned with Looney Toon cartoon characters like daffy Duck and Bugs Bunny. "I suppose we are all becoming Americanised" I said with a wry grin! Then I saw the long runway stretching out into the sea from Cristofero Colombo airport. In fact I thought we were about to land in the sea as the plane touched down. I stepped out onto the tarmac not knowing what I would find but it felt so good to be home. I was even tempted to kiss the ground as the Pope always does! I took the crowded bus from the airport to the Principe railway station and was booked into a single room in a nearby hotel. How refreshing it was to see the old station again, it hadn't changed a bit! The hotel was nothing special, but it was a base for my exploration. Looking at Cinzia once more I shook my head and told her how difficult it had been step out of the door and to make my way to Vico Nievo.

The City had changed so much. Genoa was more vibrant and pulsed with modernity. Now the port was dominated by tourists that crowded into the square, which was paved where once a road had stood, at Caricamento. The Palazzo San Giorgio was as magnificent as ever but I wondered how anyone could see the mural of Saint George slaying the dragon when the motorway now obscured its view from the sea! Where we would once have thrown stones into the water there was now a huge aquarium built in the shape of a giant blue ship. There was an old pirate ship that had once been a film set and a jib, looking like giant white fingers that groped their way out of water, with a scenic lift. The square was full of costumed models standing still and looking like statues as tourists willingly threw their money into their baskets[45]. This was nothing like the Genoa I had left behind. Even the old lighthouse was obscured by an elevated motorway

---

[45] It is worth noting that Genoa today has a healthy tourist trade that was not there in the immediate post war years.

that ran the length of the seafront. Music filled the air and the scene had made me dizzy as everyone seemed to be in a rush. My first call was to look for the Gatto Morto but I couldn't find it. My memory had faded to its exact location but I am sure that it was now a restaurant serving the hordes of tourists that passed its door. This place of notoriety had finally become respectable. At this point Cinzia could only look away as if in shame.

"I couldn't help it Tino. I know it was wrong" her eyes watering from the painful memories that betrayed her sadness.

"I was desperate. We needed money and I didn't earn enough to look after my sick mother" her words sounding hasty as she spoke. "Everyone was so poor after the war and there were few jobs. At first I thought it would be easy to earn money and then get out! But they had me Tino. They controlled me!" Her words trembled as she spoke. It was though everything had happened just the day before! With regret she said that she would change everything if only she could live that time again. The only reassurance I could offer her was to say that we had all made mistakes in the past and we can only change our futures and learn from our errors. Marco had once told me that the first time you make a mistake it isn't stupid. The second time you make the mistake – then it is stupid! I am sure that he was referring to serving customers in his restaurant but his words have stayed with me.

Entering the Carrugi that day had been very difficult for me. The streets looked exactly the same and poverty was still to to be seen. Now there were people trying to sell you cigarettes and I noticed that in the same alleyways there were prostitutes, leaning against the walls as they had done when I was a boy, and probably following in their mother's footsteps. Some of the shutters looked as though they had never been painted since I left and I felt as though I had never been away. I made my way over the uneven cobbled pavement until I finally saw that old gas lamp, still fixed solidly to the wall, like it was a welcoming beacon for my homecoming, a sentinel for Vico Nievo! I was standing on the corner of my street once more. Now I felt afraid like a schoolboy lacking in confidence! I wasn't sure what to do but I had to stand once more at my front door. Then my imagination and sentimentally took over and I imagined all of my friends playing right there in the street. I heard Davide laughing, Alfredo trying to look macho, Diego giving out his philosophies on the meaning of life and Massimo pushing and shoving Davide in a silly game. I now had a smile on my face and all because of those wonderful memories. "The boys were calling me back" I mumbled at its absurdity but it had given me the courage to take a first step back into the street. After a few short steps I stood before my old green door and I was thinking about who might live there now.

"And then......" I spoke in a more confident tone as I broke my story "as if by fate, I heard you call my name". I was amazed that Cinzia could even recognise me after so many years. "My hair is as white as snow now!" I said laughing.

"I just knew it was you Tino. I knew that one day I would see you again at that door!" She spoke as though she had waited for this moment all of her life and finally her premonition had come true!

"Then fate it must have been Cinzia. If you hadn't been looking out of your window at that moment ..." But Cinzia believed in fate and how some things were meant to be. My story was now complete and I sat back into the chair with a contented smile on my face. Cinzia frowned for a second and said "Tino, there are things you don't know yet and I will tell you them all right now" I was intrigued at what she was about tell me thinking there could be little more to say. "Now" she said in a commanding voice "it is my turn to talk to you!"

Cinzia moved a small stool close to my chair, and now sitting by my side; she clasped my hand between her hands, which comforted me as she spoke with a tender and somewhat nervous voice. For a moment the room dimmed as the sun dipped behind a cloud and the rays that came through the opened window disappeared for a while. Then suddenly the room brightened up again and Cinzia's hesitation was broken with a question. "Did you know how close your mother and I became after you left?" Of course I had no idea as her letters never really gave much away. "She confided in me a lot and became my advisor and my friend Tino!" I was in truth relieved to hear of the relationship and I was eager to understand what happened in the months that followed our escape. "Your mother" she hesitated again "had a simple philosophy. If no-one knew the whole truth about the killing of Saverio then hiding you from the mob would be a lot easier". This sounded good logic to me. "However" she said forcefully "she broke her own pledge!" Naturally, I needed to know how that was possible, and Cinzia told me that our dear mother had become too trustworthy of those close to her. She had started to confide in friends about our whereabouts and broke the rules that she had laid down herself!. Diego would ask regularly if she had heard anything from us and one day, having total trust in our old school friend, she told him everything and begged him not to tell a living soul. Unfortunately two of Saverio's cousins, the Carlito brothers, an unsavoury couple of hard and ruthless mobsters, started asking questions and they started with the boys in the street. One had grabbed at Diego, in front of the others, and he just talked and talked, begging them not to harm him. Diego was terrified and thought they would do him serious harm! All the while Alfredo and Massimo were screaming at him to be quiet, but he panicked. When the Carlito brothers, who had vowed to avenge Saverio's death, had left, Diego ran from the street in tears shouting "I am sorry, I am sorry". Alfredo called him a coward and even vowed to scar his face so that whenever he looked in the mirror he would remember how he had betrayed his friends! The other boys never ever spoke to him again and neither of them attended his untimely funeral in Milan. Unfortunately, it was too late to stop the brothers from making the trip to Sardinia that very same evening. The boys had been too ashamed and afraid to say anything until it was too late and the Carlito's arrived by ferry in Porto Torres the following morning. I thought for a while of Diego, not thinking for one minute it could have been him that gave us away, and I told Cinzia that I would have attended his funeral and that I forgave him. Time had wearied me of that terrible time.

So I now knew the identity of those two thugs. They were cousins of the loathsome Saverio that had threatened our beloved Rafaelle. They were indeed a frightening pair and Rafaelle had shown great courage to stand up to them. "You don't know how bad they treated him Tino" Cinzia's words shook me a little and I needed to know more. "One of them cut his face with a knife! Then they threatened his family if ever he breathed a word of it". At this I wanted to be sick. Rafaelle had never deserved anything as appalling as this. The thought of it made me lose my breath a little and I was angry. "If I had known this" I said "I would have returned and fought them both" Cinzia interrupted "And they would have killed you Tino!" She interrupted before I could say any more. She then told me how Rafaelle had known the full circumstances of why we fled to Sardinia and that came as a surprise. I always wondered how much of the story he actually knew. He never ever questioned me about it and believed our innocence without judgment.

"If things were different I would have followed Carla to Italy. If only ..." Cinzia sighed at my words "She knew too Tino". At this point I was on my feet and staring at Cinzia with a stare of disbelief. I stood back for a second and shook my head in bewilderment. "What do you mean she knew?" I demanded!

"She knew everything Tino. Not at first, but later"

"How?" my voice now raised. I was stunned that someone so far away could know more than I ever did.

Her words left me shocked and I felt a little betrayed that no-one spoke to me or involved Carla in something I didn't want her to hear! I listened intently as Cinzia told me a series of events that I knew nothing about. Apparently, Rafaelle had seen us both one evening sitting under a tree in the rain. He realised that we might be getting serious and he became concerned that Carla was moving back to the mainland and that I might follow. And so, he made it his mission to speak to Carla at the first opportunity he could get. Then one evening he saw her in the square and offered to buy her a coffee at the bar there. As they sat outside of the small bar Rafaelle told her how you had escaped in fear of your lives after the two of you were involved in the killing of a gangland pimp! She had confessed to Rafaelle that she was falling in love me and wanted to return to Sardinia but he had insisted that there was no future for you both and that the dangers were very real! She became afraid, not just for herself, but for her family too. The day we said goodbye was a day I thought would be a temporary parting but for Carla it really was goodbye. As she told the story I moved over to the window and looked down on the street below. There was a young couple cuddling and laughing in a doorway and thoughts of Carla came flooding back to me. Now I felt depressed, my eyes welled up and a solitary tear ran down my cheek!

"She loved you very much Tino" she said with a comforting smile though it didn't help!

"I have thought about her every day Cinzia and compared her with every girl I ever met" The sadness was apparent in my voice. Rafaelle had destroyed my one chance of love and I knew nothing about it. I wondered how different things might have been if I had returned earlier to find her. Then, a further revelation shook me even further. I learned that Carla had been to see my mother right here in Vico Nievo. They got on so well and my mother really liked her! Carla had told her that she was confused because she had met someone else but thought often of me. Even Cinzia had spoken with her and said that "she was a beautiful girl". Carla left Genoa and married and nothing was ever heard of her again. It was so hard to believe that Carla had been here in Genoa, right here in my street, and I was sailing off to America. At this point I cursed Rafaelle and hit my fist hard on the window ledge. Cinzia put a comforting arm around me and said that the old man had only done what he thought was right at the time. "Perhaps" she said "he didn't understand the depth of the love that had grown between you". I sighed and sat down once more.

Looking up I asked "did anyone else know? What about Marco in New York?" Cinzia then told me that Marco's brother, a priest, also knew exactly what had happened. That was why he asked his own brother for asylum in America. Raffaelle had been scarred for life by the Carlito brothers and Father Bartholomew took pity on what had happened to him. Marco also knew the full story and that accounted for his hostility toward Davide when we first met him. Marco, for some time, held Davide responsible for everything that had happened! Over time however he had grown close to Davide but, at least in the initial months in New York, he spoke very little with him.

I drew a deep breath and sat down once more with a sigh. Cinzia now changed the subject to her story once more "I was desperate to join you both in Sardinia after Saverio died" she said. "I had a sick mother to look after and the Carlito's just took over from where Saverio had left off". She told me that she had found comfort in my mother and that she could find no release from the lifestyle she was forced into and had even contemplated suicide. The Gatto Morto became far more notorious after Saverio died. The Carlito became involved in drugs, which was now a huge problem in Italy. One evening there was a police raid. The Carlito's were seen being dragged out by plain clothed policemen and after a few months the bar was forcibly closed. The doors and shutters were nailed shut and it stayed that way for months! Both of the brothers were given lengthy prison sentences for drug dealing and even murder. They were never heard of again. This, for Cinzia, was her release and she was free to follow a normal life after that. She had grown into middle age without marrying and then married late. "I have a son" she said with a broad grin. "I called him Davide, and he now runs the small cafe bar under the gas lamp at the corner of the street, come on Tino, let's go for a walk". As I stood up I felt a little dizzy and shaken from the revelations that I had heard and I was shocked at how much Cinzia had known. In Sardinia everything outside of Suni might well have been on another planet. Yet so many people were constantly thinking about us and worrying and caring. My mother, Tobia, Alfredo, Diego and Massimo were all long gone. Apart from Diego's early demise the others had lived full lives and raised a family here in the Carrugi. I wanted to go to the cemetery at Staglieno and to meet their children. I had so many stories to tell them all. But first I had to meet Cinzia's son.

We stepped back out onto the street and Cinzia reminded me of how she used to sit on the pavement and talk to us as children. She looked down at the very spot we would sit and chat and she smiled a childish smile. Her arm through mine we walked across the cobbles to the lamp that sat proudly over the bar on the corner. I hadn't noticed earlier but the bar was now called Davide's. "He would have liked that!" I said. Outside there were a few tables and two blue shades gave cover from the hot sun. People were sat outside drinking espresso or cappuccino and it looked a nice place to while away an evening. "We" she said "just grew too old to do everything. But my husband still likes to prepare food there. He's a wonderful man and a great cook too!" I hadn't even thought to ask about her husband. Not knowing if he would even be alive. As we approached the bar a young man came out, about in his mid thirties. He had thinning hair, was tall, slim. And a he had big cheeky smile. "Ah" he greeted us "mama". Cinzia, holding my arm tightly said "this is Davide and this is my long lost friend Tino". Davide stepped back as if he had seen a ghost. "You mean THE Tino? The one you have spoken of a million times?" Cinzia chuckled "the very one!" More relaxed now I questioned how I ever managed to fill their conversations over the years and with that I was being led by them both through the doors and into the bar.

Sitting in the corner with his back to us was an old white haired man, though he had little hair to speak of and he was slouched over the table. He had a newspaper laid across the table in front of him and a half empty glass of orange juice in his hand. Cinzia leaned into me and whispered "I named my son after his father!" The old man turned and stared for a few moments and then broke into the most recognisable of smiles. I was overcome with emotion and lost for words. "Dad, Tino has come home" his son said. The old man stood to his feet and was shaking from head to foot. He ambled, for walking would be inappropriate to describe his movement, toward me with arms outstretched. I did the same and we embraced each other as though our lives would end right there and then. Tears ran down my cheeks and I tried to speak but was too choked to make any sense. Then he moved back with hands on my shoulders. Through tears of joy he told me that he had never dared to imagine this day would ever come. "I'm not letting you go again Tino. You stay right here in Genoa" he said with a voice like an apologetic child after being scolded. Then he threw his arms around my neck and hugged me once again! "I won't leave again my old friend" I replied, at which Cinzia and young Davide joined our circle in a family embrace that seemed to last forever. We cried and we laughed together the whole evening. He told me that whilst living in San Diego he had started to suffer depression and loneliness. One day, while crossing a busy road, he was struck by a bus and suffered terrible leg injuries. He confessed that everyone thought it was an accident but it was a feeble attempt at suicide. Davide had reached the lowest point in his life at that moment and I wasn't around to help him!

My hand was rested on his shoulder as he recounted these events. But that had been enough for him to return. The Gatto Morto was thankfully closed by then and Davide was free to pursue the one woman he really loved; Cinzia. We sat there all evening talking and drinking and laughing and there were lots of tears.

After such an emotional evening I decided that I needed to walk back to my hotel and that I needed time alone to contemplate all that had happened that day. I planned to walk via the Carrugi, look at those black market stalls that sell everything from cigarettes to pornographic DVDs, look at the old port at night and stand fearlessly in front of the Gatto Morto. I wanted to stand before that bar as one who had triumphed over evil! I felt young again, happy and finally at peace with the world. Coming home was the best thing that I ever did.

We made a lunch appointment for the following day and I waved as I left them both holding each other. They told me I was family now and that was what I wanted to hear. I stepped out into the street and looked up at the old gas lamp and smiled as though it were an old friend. I needed to see my old front door again and I strolled down the street toward it. As I stood before that old door again I picked at the flaking green paint that had curled under the Italian sun. I turned for a second and noticed Cinzia and Davide at their door, arm in arm, watching me as I went, and I smiled once more, nodding in approval. We had been young teenagers after the war, growing up in a world of poverty and deprivation. It had been a time when ruthless people exploited the weak. But it was also time of bonding and great friendships that lasted a lifetime. As I strolled away from my old house I saw Diego as a thirteen year old boy "welcome home Tino" he said before fading into the dim light of the gas lamp. "I forgive you Diego" I said under my voice. Then Alfredo appeared "about time" he said and I smiled. I thanked my old friend for his loyalty and he too disappeared in to the darkness of night. Massimo was there too to welcome me "you should have come home sooner Tino. We all missed you" then he too

Senso Unico

was gone. "I missed you all too" I murmured. Then I gazed once more at 44c Vico Nievo with its flaky green painted door. I was home at last!

Some things never change. The street was still too steep to walk on, and the old port was still visible between the murky buildings. Only I had changed.

The End

In the research for this book and support I would like to thank the following: Davide Moriconi, Ian Ashcroft, Jim Connor, Virgilio Tedde and Andi and Kate Robinson,